Rock, Paper, Scissors

Reflections of Life

By J. Lew

Rock, Paper, Scissors
Reflections of Life
By J. Lew

Printed in the United States of America

ISBN 9781946806000

Scripture quotations taken from the King James Version (KJV) – *public domain*

www.jlew-books.com

Dedication

I am grateful for the many things that God has provided for me, and my wife is at the top of those blessings. With her kind and forgiving heart she continues to give, even when it comes down to her last. Her love for God and tireless work ethics have provided for the family, especially when the chips were down.

And to all the spouses that are there for one another through thick and thin.

To God be the glory.

Table of Contents

Dedication vi

Introduction ix

The Journey Home 1

A Blast to the Past 12

No More Training Wheels 16

Coming of Age 28

Getting In Shape.. 39

Renewed Spirit... 52

Final Conflict.. 65

Blurred Lines 70

Introduction

Are we willing to wait for an answer?

When we fast and pray, there are times we tend to get a little impatient waiting for the answers to our prayers. It's amazing how God is able to answer the prayers of the righteous, and what's even more amazing is how many requests in prayers he hears from the righteous and unrighteous. I am often reminded of an old saying, "He may not come when you want him, but when he comes, he's right on time." Far too often, we cut God off and move on.

We believe we're putting our best foot forward when we set out to achieve our goals. When life finally changes for us, we seldom look to God and thank him for delivering us and blessing us in our times of need. Why is that? The reason is simple — no patience! We believe after years of struggling, and after losing our homes and cars, and after going through divorces and so much more, that when our ship comes in, God had nothing to do with it. Many believe that when they were in the valley of life struggling to make it up the hill, God was not present. Now that they've made it to the top of the hill, everybody expects them to give God the glory and the credit.

Two things are at work here. First, there are times when

God allows things to happen in our lives and none of it seems fair. There are times when a builder comes to a house in disrepair; he examines the house, the foundation, and then determines how best to go about the renovations. When he finishes examining the condition of the house, he'll begin the removal of all the worn and damaged boards, and will remove the walls that restrict and obstruct the flow of the home. Then he'll add to the framework and foundation to strengthen it and everything else that makes the house function as a home. When the builder finishes the remodeling, the end result is a home envied by many. Simply put, before God can rebuild there must be a process of tearing down.

Second, I love the poem "Footprints in the Sand" by Mary Stevenson: "When we trust in God **we never walk alone**." Daniel prayed and fasted for twenty days without results, but on the twenty-first day he received his answer (Daniel 10). When we fast and pray for three days, we are often weakened with doubt, hunger, and the many other things that make us go no farther than those three days. As a result, many go away wondering if it was worth it. What do you think God would have done if Daniel had packed it up and gone about his business after three days? It's really not an answer I want to know, but I'm glad Daniel set the example for us to follow.

When we set our hearts to seek God in prayer, we should believe he has already answered and go away looking for our answer no matter how long it takes. What I'm saying is when you pray, pray with faith, hope, and belief that God is able to do what you ask him to do. No matter what you do, NEVER STOP PRAYING (I Thessalonians 5:17). The scripture says God heard Daniel's prayer the first day he set his heart to understand (Daniel 10:12), so we should understand that the angels of God aren't just fighting for you; they are fighting for the millions of others who are praying and fasting for answers as well.

The question is, "How long are you willing to wait?"

God is not blind!

God loves us, and no matter what we are going through He has a plan for our lives. I hope you believe that, because it's true, although it's hard to see that plan at times. When we are going through hard times, it feels as though our prayers are going unanswered; the wicked seem to prosper, and there you are doing everything you can possibly do to simply live from paycheck to paycheck. The question God hears all day, every day is "Where was God when...?"

God is not blind and He is not an uncompassionate God. He sees how you are treated, and He can see everything you are going through. He also sees the times when the lines of your life are blurred and there's no difference between what you are doing to others, and what the wicked are doing. It's not hard to get swept up in the world of mischief. Remember the parable of the servant who was forgiven of all, but he himself was not willing to forgive (Matthew 18: 23-35). When God has taken away our grief and helped us to move on in life, it profits us nothing to harbor ill will toward those who treated us with gall or owe us and cannot repay their debt.

Allow God to clean and polish our cobwebbed temples, and go out and help those who truly want to be helped. Pray without ceasing and ask Him to keep you from the things He took away from you. Don't let those who despise you pull you back into the fray of that old you. Again, we are reminded that it is not impossible to turn back to the things of our former selves. The parable of the unclean spirit that has GONE OUT of a man (Matthew 12: 43-45) reminds and warns us of this. If God has cleaned and garnished your temple, why is it empty? When the old self comes calling, it should find stiff and unrelenting resistance.

Every day there is someone being abused and tormented, and yet when they are delivered they find the strength and love to forgive their tormentors. I'm not saying that we possess some super ability to block every wrong thought that comes to the mind; the devil sifts us all day looking for a weakness, minute by minute, and when he finds it he exploits it as he did to Jesus, Job, David, Joseph, and many others throughout time. The devil will continue until the new heavens and new earth are revealed.

God's eyes are not just on the sparrows and lilies in the field, but they are forever focused on those he cares for the most... YOU.

Summer of 1940

A group of boys are starting a game of stickball, and they are choosing who will play on which team. Michael's father is walking home after working his Saturday shift and sees the group of young boys; they look about the same age as his son. He walks into the house and greets his wife with a kiss and a hug, and then asks, "Where's Michael?"

"He's in the backyard playing," his wife answers.

So he walks out to the backyard, where Michael is playing with his toy truck. When he looks up and sees his father, Michael runs up and hugs him.

"Michael," he says, "There are some boys in the street about to put together a team for a game of stickball. Why don't you go out there and join them? They look about your age, around eight or so. Go out there and have fun."

Excited, Michael runs through the house, out the front door, and into the street where the team selections have just begun.

"Can I play?" he asks.

The boys turn around, and there standing in front of them is a skinny kid with big black-rimmed glasses and his trousers pulled up just under his chest. Craig Daniels laughs and asks, "Who's the wiener?"

"I think he lives three houses down; he doesn't come out that often," Tony remarks. Waving him on, he says, "Sure kid, come on. We haven't chosen sides yet."

"What's your name?" Jimmy asks.

"Michael Oliver James III."

Some of the boys are bending over holding their stomachs while others are poking fun of his trousers and glasses.

Then Craig asks Michael, "Do you know how to play stickball?"

Michael nods and says, "Yes." Craig tells him he's only allowed to play on Tony's team.

"No," Tony yells, pointing his finger at Craig. "That's not fair. It shouldn't matter whose team he plays on."

Craig pushes Tony and says, "Let's settle this then. We'll play Rock, Paper, Scissors, and whoever loses gets the little wiener."

Tony protests, but plays the game anyway. "We'll start on three, okay? One, two, three," they say, pounding a fist into their palms.

"Yes!" Craig yells. "Rock beats scissors, you lose. You get the wiener."

Chapter 1
The Journey Home

So *much has changed*, Mike thinks. *Even the highways.* "Fifty years ago this used to be a two-lane road with no shoulder, and most of it was gravel; now it's a four-lane highway," he says, talking to himself. The old landmarks have all eroded over time, leaving nothing but old dilapidated buildings that remind him he is either lost or headed in the right direction on the wrong highway.

Mike wonders what town he's passed, because most of the new highways bypassed them. He murmurs, "I have to pay close attention; otherwise I will pass up the old town."

He drifts into thought. *When I left home in 1950, we traveled down Highway 287. This is the first time I have traveled on Highway 183 and its many exchange highways; it's supposed to be a shorter route.*

In the middle of Mike's thoughts, his cellphone rings. "Hey pretty girl," he answers.

Jackie, his wife, returns the greeting. "Hey man of mine, how's the drive?"

"A little longer than I remember. I went through Lubbock about twenty miles ago. I should be getting pretty close; the map reads another twelve miles, and I should be exiting the highway to the old farm road that leads into town."

"Well, I was just calling to make sure you're okay."

"I'm okay, just getting a little tired," he reassures her.

"If you need to pull over you should to stretch your legs," she says.

"I'm doing okay," Mike replies. "I should be there pretty soon."

"I was thinking about when we and the kids traveled to the Grand Canyon. Now that was a long drive. Took us a couple of days to get there, I remember."

"Driving does bring back old memories." She says.

"Ha, yes," he says.

"Well, don't pass your exit." She warns.

"I'm pretty focused on the signs." He explains. "I just passed one that says my exit is six miles ahead."

"Well, I'm going to let you drive, okay? I love you, and be careful." She says.

"All right, I'll call you after I check into the hotel. Love you too, bye." Then Mike hangs up.

"Cellphones," he says aloud. "Wow, talk about changes; we were happy to have party lines." Then Mike thinks back to when he grew up. *I can remember catching my mother listening to Mrs. Mays's conversations on many occasions. Mrs. Mays was one of those nosey neighbors who seemed to know all the gossip in town. If you ever wanted to know something, all you had to do was be in her inner circle, or be connected on a party line with her. I knew my mom was listening to the hottest gossip because she held the dishtowel over the phone's mouthpiece. And they wondered how everybody knew everybody's business!*

Mike laughs at the thought of being driven out of the house so that his mother could continue her snooping.

In about four miles, Mike should exit on the right. Exiting from the highway onto the feeder road, he comes to a stop sign. He turns left onto the road to Thumperville after briefly stopping. Then, after a half-mile on the road, he runs over a pothole and things begin to look and feel the same as they did fifty years ago. There are miles of cornfields on both sides of the road, and old houses with collapsed roofs or roofs that look like old swayback horses. Mike thought back to when he was a kid sitting in the backseat looking at the power lines; how they rolled from pole to pole, just rolling with the Texas hills, up and down like a roller coaster. He would sit deep in thought for some reason, just staring at those rolling power lines every time they hit the road.

Sitting at a stop sign on the edge of town, Mike has arrived at his destination, Thumperville. He drives up to the hotel, pulls into the parking lot, and parks the car. Stretching in his seat, he looks about before getting out.

"Well, old boy, you're here," Mike says to himself.

He gets out and stretches again, and then looks around at what seems like a time capsule: the old two-tank service station that no longer has an attendant; Doc. Jacobs's pharmacy across the street, or what used to be his pharmacy; Hadley's farming and feed store; Dailey's Grocer; a paint and body shop that used to be Silva's Garage; the city's police department, the city council building, and the fire department next to the cornfield at the end of the road.

Mike laughs and shakes his head, thinking, *I wonder if any of the firemen have problems getting to sleep, lying awake at night wondering who's in the cornfield? And the question at dinner is, "Does corn come with the menu?"* He grabs his luggage from the backseat and walks through the door to check in.

"Good afternoon to ya," says the attendant at the front desk. "You look a little tired."

"Just a little," Mike replies.

"Where ya coming from?" she asks.

"Austin."

"Well, you should be tired," she says. "That's about a six-hour ride."

"Seven, but who's counting?" laughs Mike.

"Well sugar, who should I say is checking in today?" she laughs back.

"Mr. James, Michael James."

"Okay... I see you'll be staying two nights with us; will that be one key or two?"

"One will do fine."

"Could I see the credit card you used to book the room?"

"Sure," and Mike hands her his card and shows her his driver's license.

"Thank you, hon. Are you here for the high school's fiftieth reunion?"

"I am, and at my age, I wonder if we could hold this reunion in a small conference room. There were only twenty-eight of us who graduated in 1950. And I've been a little out of touch with everyone, so I'm not sure how many of us will show up."

"Well it seems to be enough to hold the event in the high school gym. I hear they have it all decorated, with the stage set up for you folks."

"That's good to hear."

"Most of the men brought their wives, while some brought their other half, if you know what I mean."

Mike smiles as she hands him back his card.

"You'll be in room 215, a few doors away from the elevator."

"Thank you." He said.

He takes his key and walks to the elevator. When the door opens a couple of kids walk out with towels draped over their shoulders, heading toward the pool. The elevator lumbers to the second floor and the door opens. Mike steps into the hallway, onto the green carpet with decorative colors swirling together in a random pattern. Walking slowly down the hall, he scans each room number for 215. Then, stopping outside his room, he pushes the key card into the lock slot and opens the door. There's a queen-size bed in the middle of the room with a nightstand on either side, a dresser across the floor by the foot of the bed, and a thirty-two-inch television. Mike turns the television on and finds he has to wait until it warms up before the picture comes on. He drops everything on the bed and goes to the bathroom to find two large towels, two hand towels, and two face towels on a rack on the wall in front of the toilet, and a bathtub with the curtain open. When he's finished, he goes to the sink to wash his face and hands with one of the two bars of soap placed on the side. A small coffee maker and a couple of disposable cups wrapped in plastic accompany an ice bucket with no top. With his hands washed and dried, Mike walks over to the bed and sits at the edge where the picture has finally joined the audio. The room is clean as far as he can see; then he looks at the clock, which reads 2:23 p.m. It comes to mind that he should call Jackie to let her know he's made it to the hotel safe and sound. Instead he lies back on the bed.

Jackie didn't want to come back to the old town; she put it behind her when they went off to college. Not long after they graduated from Thumperville High School, her mother remarried and moved to Arizona. Mike's parents moved to Houston while he and Jackie were still attending Southwest Texas State Teachers College after his father had a mild stroke while visiting his brother Elmer in Houston. Elmer was Mike's father's older brother, and they decided it would be better if they were closer to a good hospital in case other medical emergencies came up.

In their junior year of college, Mike and Jackie tied the knot and rented an apartment. After graduating, they started their teaching careers in San Marcos. Then, after their second year in the area, in the summer of 1956, he and Jackie celebrated the birth of Michael Oliver James IV, their first child. Jackie did not teach that year, while Mike continued to teach math and science. The following summer, they decided to move to Austin and teach at separate schools. Mike and Jackie had been living in Austin for two years when Jackie got pregnant with their second child, a daughter they would name Patricia Marie James. That summer Mike started working for a small nursery to make extra money in the lean summer months when they were off, and Jackie took work at the library. In 1961, Simon Andrew James, named after Jackie's father, was born; and three years after that Anthony Everest James, or little Tony, came into the world. After the Vietnam War ended in 1975, and the country was just short of being at peace, Jackie and Mike, now with four children, moved from South Austin to Northwest

Austin. At nineteen, Michael was a physics major at the University of Texas; Patricia was sixteen, Simon fourteen, and Tony eleven. Jackie was a principal at her school, while Mike continued to teach math and science at one of the few private schools in Central Texas. When Tony entered the Air Force in 1985, Mike and Jackie decided to retire after thirty years of public service. And after a year off, Jackie decided to write books for a living and Mike decided to open a small nursery to keep busy. One evening while sitting on the couch, he mentioned to Jackie, "Growing plants seems to be a lot easier than growing children. You know, they don't talk back, and they don't wreck your car in the middle of the night and park it back in the drive like nothing ever happened."

She laughed and said, "And they don't leave home climbing out the window and then climbing into their girlfriend's window either."

"How did we survive?" asked Mike.

"I don't know," Jackie replied, "but now it's their turn to raise their own kids and see what it's like to be a parent.

"Oh yes, do you remember the famous 'You don't understand line' we heard from all four of the kids at one time or another? I'm still waiting for one of them to explain what it is we don't understand. And how is it that they let the oldest talk them into doing some of the craziest things?"

"Which one of those crazy things are you referring to?" she asked.

"The one I had in mind was when Simon climbed up on the roof and was too afraid to get down after he got up there. Then I had to stand underneath him and convince him that I could catch him if he jumped. I wasn't sure if I was convincing him I would catch him or convincing myself that if he jumped I could actually catch him."

Laughing, Jackie said, "What was it our nineteen-year-old Tony said when we explained to him the importance of saving his money after he finally started working?"

"'I don't make enough to save'? I'm still puzzled with that one. The car he drove is mine, he had no bills to pay, we weren't asking for a dime, and he 'didn't make enough money to save'? Goodness gracious... are you serious?"

Jackie grinned and said, "How about Pat's famous line? 'I'm not a kid anymore, I'm thirteen.'"

Mike laughed and remarked, "Don't forget the many times I asked Mike to rake the yard after he cut it, and he would tell me that none of his friends had to rake their parents' yards. There are times when you raise children you just want to scream to high heaven."

They both leaned back on the couch and looked at each other and laughed.

"I guess we wouldn't change a thing, would we?" asked Mike.

"Not a single day," Jackie replied, and then she kissed him.

Mike smiles at the thought of reminiscing while he lies down on the bed, looking up at the popcorn ceiling. He tries to take a short nap before he has to travel to the school for the first day of the reunion. Rolling over onto his side, he pulls out the invitation from the trip folder he prepared before he left. Pat printed out the invitation for him; she found out about the high school's fiftieth reunion from a friend whose dad has family in Thumperville. The time to be there is 5:30 p.m., so Mike sets the clock for 4:30 and drifts off to sleep.

After a short nap that seems to have only lasted a few minutes, Mike gets up and begins to go through the luggage Jackie packed for him. He sees she packed the Lysol, his own bar of soap, and some cleansers for the bathroom. Of course this was standard for when they traveled with the kids. The only thing missing was the... *Oh, never mind,* he thought. The toilet seat covers. And then Mike thought to himself, *I'm sure she intended for me to use these things before I went into the bathroom and used it. I guess I'll spray the tub and scrub the toilet seat when I get back.*

After getting dressed Mike walks out of the room, making sure the door locks behind him. Outside the heat from the sun is scorching and there are no clouds in the sky. Looking around again, he starts to think back on the days long passed. He climbs into the car and turns the AC on high. Sitting only for a few seconds, he adjusts the vents to cool himself off faster. Backing out, Mike leaves the hotel, turning left to drive down the road he walked for many years. He didn't have a car until after he and Jackie got married during their junior year of college. *I have a little time*, he thinks, so he turns left on 7th Street, which leads to his parents' old house on Avenue D. Passing the park he'd dubbed the Park of Tears, he can see it isn't what it was in the past. Mike figures most of the kids are at home playing with their game consoles. Their youngest child Tony would play with his Atari on TV or watch his favorite shows all day. In their day, most of Mike and Jackie's time was spent outside; and when they didn't have anything to do, they listened to the radio.

Mike pulls up and parks across the street from his old house. He observes the newly landscaped yard; the house is painted gray with the post on the porch painted white. The old shutters on the side of the windows are all gone and they've poured a concrete drive. He grabs his camera and gets out of the car and takes six snapshots of the house at different angles. *Changes*, he thinks, and gets back in the car and drives on. Mike's next stop is Jackie's old house on 9th Street. He finds there have been great improvements there also and takes snapshots to show her when he gets home from his trip. Then Mike moves on and drives back to the highway, traveling on and passing the street for the school. He stops by the old drive-in theater that used to show the best movies ever. It's just a shell of itself now, sitting on the outskirts of town right off the highway past 22nd Street. Mike drives onto the theater grounds and gets out to take pictures of the old ghost of a parking lot and the building that once served the best popcorn, hotdogs, and soda. He walks slowly back to the car with a smile and drives down to where Sam's Drive-In Cafe used to be; it was the old hangout and the place to go and see the hottest cars and carhop girls. A car dealership is there now, but down the road Mike can see there is a Sonic's Drive-In. *It's not the same.*

Turning left on 16th Street, he knows he is coming up to the school. More potholes and there's the old school... Thumperville High. Turning left into the parking lot, Mike drives through another pothole; he's paying attention to the school building... and more potholes he has to drive around. He finds a parking space for his 1998 silver Mercedes S 350 facing the old gym. He can see who's who as they arrive. There aren't many cars here yet, so he waits for his classmates to show up to see if he can recognize them from his high school days. Anxiety begins to build, and he thinks back over the fifty years since he and Jackie left: a marriage, four kids, and retirement.

Mike never thought he'd ever be back at this school again. His fiftieth high school reunion — where had all that time gone since he graduated? He begins to think, *I drove all this way and now I'm sitting here wondering if I should even get out of the car?* Looking at the school, Mike considers how it could use a little paint and some new bricks, and the parking lot and street could use a little more asphalt. He watches as a purple Ford racing across the school lot, driving through every pothole and double-parking. *Well, well, well, some things never change,* Mike thinks. *Craig Daniels still drives reckless and parks across two spaces near sideways.* Laughing, he watches Craig pry himself out of his rented Ford. *I take that back, some things have changed. Looks like he'll need two chairs to double-park himself at the table.* "Humph," Mike grunts, "I was wondering where all the time went? From where I sit, it just wobbled into the gym." As more cars drive up, he can see everyone in their Sunday go-to meeting dress walking into the old gym. Man, he can hardly remember any of these people.

"What am I doing here?" Mike asks himself. His heart begins to race, and anxiety runs rampant, changing his current state of mind. His hands start to shake. Mike wipes the sweat from his face, and then takes a deep breath to calm himself. He closes his eyes and covers them with his hand, which is now sweating as well. Exhaling slowly, Mike sighs, and then takes another deep breath and lowers his hands from his face. *No, no, you've got to be kidding me*, he thinks as his mind struggles to make sense of all this. He slowly looks up with his eyes, keeping his head lowered, and then peers down at his hands. That voice — that game — and out of the corner of his eye, he sees him, and looks up... and time between times is blurred.

Chapter 2
A Blast to the Past

"Rock, Paper, Scissors." Craig Daniels and Tony Reams are dueling it out.

"Come on you two," all the boys are yelling.

"Let's play without them," shouts Wesley Edger.

"No," Craig shouts back. "Each team has to be even, five against five. Those are the rules."

"I want to play too you know," yells Bradley Dunbar. "Maybe they could play without you," he says, shoving Wesley, which causes a shoving match and chaos among the two teams until Craig grabs them both and demands they knock it off.

"Next time pick me before you pick Wesley, and then he can see how it feels standing here with him. Then he'll see how it feels."

"Get on with it so we can play," David yells.

The two team leaders continue to play Rock, Paper, Scissors; then Craig chooses rock and Tony chooses paper.

"Yes!" Tony says. "Paper covers rock — I win."

Craig demands one more round, but Tony protests and chooses Bradley. Upset, Craig grabs the football off the ground and commands his team. "Let's go," he yells, and then turns and tells Michael Oliver James III, "you better not screw up," waving his fist at him. Wesley taunts Craig, shouting across the field as they walk away to the other side. "The loser has to kick off to the winner and his team."

"I know!" Craig yells back. "I made the rules, remember?"

When they get to the other side of the field, Craig checks his line and tells his team, "I'm going to kick the ball short, and I want all of you to get on it before Tony and his boys. Do you hear me, you little wiener?"

"Yeah, you little wiener," says Twin One, pointing at Michael, "and don't be jumping on top of the pile or I'll clobber ya for sure." He pounds his fist into his hands.

On the other side of the field Tony instructs his team, telling them, "Whoever gets the ball should stay behind the blockers and run on the side where Michael is, and we will start the game with a touchdown ahead of Craig and his team." Tony looks across the field at Craig and yells, "We're ready."

Craig looks at his team and asks, "Are you guys ready?" They all respond, "Ready."

With their hands on their knees and ready to run on both sides, Craig kicks the ball almost to the middle of the field. As both sides scramble for the ball, James dives on it before his brother David does.

"That's cheating," Tony and his team yell. "You have to kick it over, and this time you have to kick it all the way downfield."

"No, I don't have to kick it again," Craig yells, and then pushes Tony to the ground. Tony jumps up, and then they wrestle and tumble on the ground while all the others are yelling for their team leader. Craig puts Tony in a headlock.

"I can do this all day, so say 'uncle' and I'll let you up."

Tony cries, "Uncle! Now get off of me." Furious, he says, "You're a cheat, Craig. You don't play fair. Is that one of your new rules?"

Craig simply replies, "We're on the offence, so get used to being on the defense while we run through you like the wind."

"You mean like a bad smelling fart," Tony yells, and both sides laugh at his remark.

Craig huddles with his team and instructs James, who is the fastest on the field, to run past Bradley so he can throw him the ball. Tony huddles with his team and tells them, "I'm going to line up in front of Michael so that I'll have a good chance at knocking Craig down on his cheating butt. When I do, he's going to want to fight, so I'm running straight home before he can catch me." Tony further instructs them, "I want everybody to pile up on Craig when he's on the ground so when he gets up, I'll already be gone."

On both sides, everybody knows what they have to do at the line. Ronald centers the ball to Craig, while James is running down the field with Bradley close by his side; as fast as Tony can run and with all his strength, he runs through Craig like a freight train. Craig's feet are off the ground and he fumbles the ball, but no one seems to be going for the ball. They are doing what Tony asked, so when Craig lands on his back with his feet over his head, and it looks like he's running in place trying to right himself and get back on his feet, Wesley, Twin Two, and David pile up on top of Craig. They try to hold him down, giving Tony a chance to run for his life. Craig swings wildly at them and demands they get off of him. Fuming, Craig stands on his feet; he sees that Tony has already run off the field, and when he turns and sees Michael, he walks angrily toward him with tight fists and his lips tucked in his mouth. Michael knows he can't outrun him or fight him, so he stands holding his arms up to protect himself while Craig punches him in the side of his head, knocking him to the ground.

"I told you what would happen if you screwed up, you little wiener," Craig reminds him. Craig then commands all the boys from both teams to follow him. The boys run off to chase after Tony, who has a great head start and is in full stride. Michael watches them in hot pursuit, hearing Craig and the others yelling at Tony as they chase him all the way to his house. Michael picks himself up off the ground, and with his head facedown and his arms limp at his side, he walks home crying.

Chapter 3
No More Training Wheels

"Rock, Paper, Scissors." The coaches play in the school gym while building a team for dodgeball. Everyone must participate in all PE activities, and dress in their t-shirts, gym shorts, socks, and sneakers. The numbers are odd, and there is always one person last to be chosen. Neither one of the coaches wants Michael on their team, so they play Rock, Paper, Scissors to see who the unlucky person will be that day. Standing straight as a rail with both feet together, Michael nervously awaits to see who the winner will be. Coach Grey draws scissors and Coach Webb draws paper... scissors cut paper. Coach Webb looks at Michael and without a word points in the direction he wants him to go. Michael runs to his position, readying himself for the onslaught of balls. All the balls are set in the middle of the court, and all the boys are ready for the scramble. Michael knows that he does not have a chance to grab any of the balls, so he devises a plan to survive past the first few seconds of the game. This time he is on the same side as Tony, and Craig is on the other side.

Tony whispers to Mike, "Try to catch Twin Two's ball! He hurt his arm playing football over the weekend."

"Okay," Michael says with a big smile on his face, and then

gives Tony a quick nod.

The whistle blows to start the game, and all the boys run toward the line of balls to be the first to grab one and scramble back to their side. Michael keeps to his original plan, lets everybody go ahead of him, stands back, and waits for the hurt to come. He stands behind another kid named Wade, and every move Wade makes in front of him he makes the same one behind him. Twin Two catches the ball that was thrown at him and Michael knows this is his time. When Twin Two sees him, he takes a few steps forward to really try to knock Michael off his feet. When Michael is in the clear, Twin Two throws the ball as hard as he can; a loud booming sound comes from the ball hitting Michael in the chest, and everybody stops when they see that Michael catches the ball.

"Jerk!" screams Twin Two. There is Michael cupping the ball in his arms.

Tony shouts, "Run," and then every ball from the other side weighs in on Michael; he is jumping, dodging, and running from one side of the court to the other, and not one ball hits him. Trying to catch his breath, he is now clear to throw the ball at someone on the other side. The coaches and most of the boys are laughing so hard at the way he ran and dodged the onslaught of balls; most of them are not paying any attention to him having the ball, so their guard is down. Michael throws the ball at the first person in front of him, but Craig runs in front of the boy and catches it. The whistle blows and the coach moves Michael off the court to the stands. Tony looks at him and gives him a thumbs-up. Michael doesn't care that Craig caught the ball; he is overjoyed that he was able to catch it for once in his life and not be the first one out. Happily, he watches most of the game from the stands.

"Rock, Paper, Scissors," Michael can hear as the game begins behind him. He does not want to look, but leans forward to try and prevent what he knows is coming. The rubber band really hurts, so he yells, "Cut it out!"

The dodgeball game is halted only for a moment while both coaches look back to see what the ruckus is in the stands. Coach Grey says, "What's going on over there?"

Michael points in the direction of a small group of boys and says, "One of them shot me in the back of the ear with a rubber band."

Both coaches turn around and blow their whistles to continue the game. Michael then moves down to the bottom of the stands directly behind Coach Grey, thinking he will be safe. Twin Two sees what the others are doing and notices the coaches did nothing to prevent them from doing it again, so he walks over and joins the group. He takes a piece of paper and folds it until it is as tight and small as a pebble. He takes the rubber band from David and stretches it as far as he can without breaking it, and then lets it go. The paper hits Michael so hard it puts a welt on the back of his neck. All he can do is scream, grab the back of his neck, and cry.

The game is halted once again, and Coach Grey tells him to go and get dressed while Coach Webb walks up the stands to the group of boys and takes the rubber band from Twin Two. He then takes the rest of the rubber bands from David and places them in his pocket. Waving his arms, he blows the whistle so that the game can continue. Michael runs to the dressing room screaming, and then runs over to the bench in front of the baskets, praying and wishing he was older and bigger so that he could beat up anyone who picked on him.

Later, Twin Two walks in and sees Michael on the bench crying and holding his neck. He walks past him and says, "Coach told me to get dressed," and then he goes to his basket and pulls it down while Michael sits on the bench doubled over with his face hidden in his hands. Twin Two gets dressed in a hurry, then puts his basket back in place and starts walking out. Stopping in front of Michael, he can see the red welt on his neck, and taps him on the arm.

"Sorry, it won't happen again," he says. "I promise." Then he walks out of the dressing room.

After the gym class, Tony catches up with Michael and asks him if he is all right. Michael lets him know that he is okay and tells him that Twin Two apologized for hitting him.

Tony says, "I think he was just upset that you caught his ball and that put him out of the game."

"Yeah, that's what I thought. Then he told me the coach sent him to the locker room to get dressed."

"No, the coach did not tell him that," Tony says. "He had the chance to play the second game, but he left and came back in his clothes. Look Mike, first of all, I know you don't want to be called Mike, but it's part of your name. And none of the guys will call you Michael Oliver James III."

Michael asks Tony, "Why does everybody always pick on me?"

"Well, it's because you look and dress like a wimp. You have to loosen up, pull your pants down under your navel, and stop holding your books like the girls do. Hold them in your hands down at your side like all the guys do and not against your chest. We're in the eighth grade now; we're grown up so we're expected to walk and act like men. This is the time when the girls really start digging us guys." Tony pulls the collar of his shirt up. "Oh, by the way, do you know that Jacquelyn Westbury girl?"

"I'm not sure," Michael replies.

"Well she knows you, and man does she have the hots for you, so you have to toughen up."

Michael says, "Tony, don't lie to me. Everybody hates me — especially the girls."

"Your screaming and running out of the gym didn't help you none with all the girls laughing at you from behind the curtains. But I'm serious, no lie, for some strange reason she really does like you."

"Who told you that?" Michael asks.

"Well she and Patricia Gale are good friends, and Pat told me to tell you she kind of likes you. She's too shy to tell you herself." Tony stops and holds Michael back, as they are in front of the men's room. "Mike, I can only help you so much, but the rest is up to you. Pull your pants down from your chest and do the same with your gym shorts when we are in the gym."

Michael has respect for Tony; he is the only one who stood up for him when everyone else was out to get him. The only thing Michael can say to him in response is "yes," and he shakes his head in agreement with everything Tony says. So he walks into the men's room, looks around at the other boys standing in front of the long trough urinals, walks past them and into the stall, and locks it. He takes a deep breath and sucks in his stomach before pulling his pants down below his navel. He looks down at his pants that are now too long, so he bends down and rolls them up to where he feels comfortable. He stands in the stall and waits until he thinks most of the boys are out of the men's room.

Slowly he unlocks the door, peering out and walking out and standing in front of the mirror. He loosens his belt so he can adjust his pants and make sure his shirt is tucked in neatly at the waist, and then he checks to see what he looks like holding his books down at his side. With a couple of nervous nods in the mirror and a quiet "cool man," he hurriedly walks out of the men's room as more boys are walking in. His spirits renewed, he walks out with a smile on his face. When the door opens and Michael walks out, Tony sees the new Mike, gives him a thumbs-up, and comments on his new look.

"That's the way we men are supposed to dress," Tony says in a hip tone. "Now you have to do something with that slicked-back hairdo you're sporting. When you get home, look in the mirror and see what style best fits you; you might try combing it to the side."

"Sure Tony," Mike replies as they walk to their next class.

"Now I want you to understand something about the guys — they won't stop pounding on you just because you pulled your pants down out of the clouds, but you will have to stand up for yourself when they pick on you. You understand what I'm saying?"

"Sure Tony."

"You may even have to punch somebody in the nose. You remember a couple of summers ago when we were just kids in the sixth grade, and I knocked Craig on his cheating butt?"

"Yes," Mike replies, "but I also remember while you were running for your life, he nearly knocked the life out of me."

"I told you I was sorry about that," Tony says while rubbing his ear. "I didn't know he was going to do that. Anyway, after that day he didn't come after me anymore. He's just a big jerk and thinks he can beat up anybody he wants when he wants, and David will do whatever he says, so I want you to watch out for him too."

"What's Craig's problem anyway?" Mike asks.

"I think it has to do with him failing the sixth grade and then the eighth grade last year. This year I think they will just pass him to get him out of the school. He's supposed to be in the tenth grade; if it wasn't for his old man being on the city council he'd probably have dropped out by now."

Holding his head down, Mike says, "I think he likes picking on people in the school. That's why he hasn't dropped out."

Tony says, "I don't know about that, but you have to start defending yourself."

"Okay, I'll do my best. You know what, Tony?"

"What?"

"When I caught that ball I stood there because I was trying to catch my breath, and you said Twin Two hurt his arm; all I saw was a lot of stars and then I heard you tell me to run, so I ran as fast as I could."

Tony is laughing. "Man, you should have seen you running. That was the fastest I have ever seen you run, and your legs looked so funny when you were jumping and dodging and holding your arms up and stuff. Man, that was the funniest thing I have ever seen in my life. You looked so skinny when you ran across the court."

"I was running for my life," Mike says.

"You know what, Mike? It probably wouldn't hurt if you ate a little more; man, you are the skinniest guy in the whole school. And why do you hunch over like an old man?"

"Don't know," Mike replies.

"You have to stop hunching so much; my parents would be screaming if I hunched over as much as you do. From now on, every time I see you hunching over like that I'm going to punch you... not hard, though," Tony tells him. "Just enough so you'll stop."

Tony sits behind Mike in class so whenever he sees Mike hunching, he pokes him in the back with his pencil. When Mike leans back, Tony tells him to sit up straight. After a few months of being told to sit up straight, Mike makes sure he sits up at home and at school.

With school out now, Mike is glad for the break; he's not running and hiding for his life from Craig and David. At home his mother is impressed with how Mike is learning to sit up straight.

"I'm impressed with the way you are sitting up at the table these days," she praises him.

"Yes," his dad says. "Son, you're really looking like a young man all grown up."

"Mike," his mother says with a worried face, "we've also noticed that you are..." She looks at her husband. "Well, your father and I are a little worried about some of your other changes."

"What other changes?" he asks.

His father says, "I know it's hard being different, but that doesn't mean you have to change who you are."

Then his mother interjects, "I want you to keep your shirt tucked in your pants at all times, and you are to button your shirt all the way up to the top button. They put those buttons on the shirt for a reason. And your hair, young man, you and your father will go to the barber shop and get your hair cut the way a respectable young man should; no son of mine will go around looking like he belongs to some gang."

"Mom, Dad, first of all, I'm not part of a gang." Mike sighs as he holds his head down. "I only have three friends, and two of them are girls who you know, and the other is Tony. Not much of a gang I'd say."

"Look son, we just don't want you hanging around with Louis Daniels's son Craig."

"Serious, Dad, all he does is beat me up and call me names and tell me the only thing you're good at is cleaning everybody's toilets. He calls me the janitor's boy, and when I say something, he punches me in the nose and stands over me. Tony is the only one who cares; he's the only one who Craig Daniels wouldn't fight."

"We care too, Michael. Your father is a hardworking man, and if it weren't for him, we wouldn't have this house and the food you're eating. Young man, you don't take that tone with him."

"Mom, Dad, I don't mean any disrespect. I defend what Dad does, but then I get beaten up after doing it." He sighs. "I'm not hungry anymore; may I be excused, please?" After a moment Mike is excused from the table. He puts his plate on the counter and walks out the back door. A few minutes later his father walks out the back door and stands by the chair he's sitting in. "Is this seat taken?" he asks. Mike looks up at him and gestures for him to sit. "You're getting it pretty hard from the fellows, are you?"

"Yes sir."

"Look Michael, your mother and I are not here to beat you up. We're your parents and we only want what is best for you, and to help you get started in the right direction. That's our job."

"I know," Mike says, "but that direction sometimes takes me down the road of nose bleeds and headaches. Don't get me wrong or anything, I'm not ungrateful, but I'm tired of getting beaten up all the time."

"I don't much blame you, son. When I served in the Army I served less than three months in the Great War because I got shot, and I lost a lung. Uneducated at nineteen, I came back home after being released from the hospital. I had to take the first job that paid — cleaning the toilets, sweeping and mopping the floors, and emptying the trash at the school, the police station, and the city hall building. There are times today I think they make an extra mess of the place just because they know I'm cleaning up behind them. I met your mother in 1925 before the Great Depression.

"She was working at the grocer and I was buying a couple of cans of pork and beans, and I was a little short on cash. I was going to put one of the cans back, but she let me have it for the little money I had in my pocket. After that we became friends. She was the most beautiful angel I had ever seen. She told me she had to come home and work to help her family during the summer months when she was not attending school. She was attending Baylor College for Women. I wasn't much on reading, so she helped me out with that and I can tell you I was really grateful for her help. In 1927 she graduated and we got married. I worked two jobs and she continued to work at the grocer until she got that teaching job at the elementary level of the school. That was before they built a separate school building. Then we had you in '32. The Depression was the hardest thing we had to face. I must have cleaned a million toilets, but I didn't care because I had two of the most beautiful people in my life I was working for. I hope you never have to experience what I went through. That's why I work so hard; I want you to get a good education and have the kind of job that I never had. There weren't many jobs here in this town for a boy with one lung and without a proper education after the Great War. When the Depression hit us, it was almost impossible for many to find work, but there was always a need for clean toilets and floors. So you see, God provided for us when many were standing in soup and bread lines. You know the story of Joseph when his brothers sold him into slavery, right?"

"Yes sir," Mike says.

"Well they did it because they were jealous of him. I ugh... can't say that there is anybody in this town or any other town that I know of who is jealous of me cleaning toilets, but I tell you, when there was no jobs there were some in this town who were jealous of me for having a job, even if it was cleaning toilets. I wasn't getting much, but it was more than what they were getting. I have always thought, 'A little bit of something is better than a whole lot of nothing.' So you see, it's like the Bible says, 'What Joseph's brothers meant for evil, God meant for good.' They sold him into slavery, and those who purchased him sold him in Egypt, but all of that was part of God's plan. So when they were having that terrible seven-year drought, and there was no food throughout all the lands, God put Joseph in a place where he was able to provide for his family and many other people all over the land. I look at what God did for me, and I took the job nobody wanted, but when we were going through the Great Depression, God put me in the type of job that allowed me to take care and provide for my family all the way up to now."

Michael's father continues. "People around these parts and all over the country lost their homes during those times. I was able to buy this house at a really good price. We pray to God every day looking to the day when this war we're in now will finally be over. God will always look after us, and your mother and I are always looking after you. Michael, I'll tell you, those were times that hurt and I mean it really hurt. I feel I'm the luckiest man in the world. I have the greatest wife a man can have and the smartest son a man can father. Your mother and I are really proud of you and we want you to know that."

They both get up from their chairs, and Michael gives his father a big hug.

"Thanks, Dad."

Chapter 4
Coming of Age

Michael walks to Tony's house because there is nothing to do at home. Tony is leaning back on the porch steps and remarks, "Man, I can't wait for school to start; I'm going to try out for the football team this year. And basketball and track."

Mike looks at him and says, "All that sounds really great, but if you don't mind, I'm in no big hurry for school to start."

"What?" Tony says as he sits up. "Don't you want to see Jacquelyn? I know her father don't let her court, but you have to want to see her."

"I see her every now and then. She walks to the park with her friends two or three times a week. We walk together and I push her on the swing and we talk until she has to leave, and then I walk her to her street and go home or come here and hang out with you."

"Tell me, Mike, have you kissed her yet?"

"Goodness no. Have you kissed Patricia?"

"We're in love, man, and people in love kiss. She's a great kisser; we've been smooching all summer."

"What's it like? Kissing, I mean."

"She has really soft lips and her body is warm against mine, and... well I can't tell you everything. You'll have to get

Jacquelyn to kiss you and you'll see for yourself what kissing is like."

"Oh, come on, you can tell me. We're best friends, remember?" Mike says in a high-pitched tone.

"Yes, well my brother told me that there are some things a man should keep to himself; he told me that when I asked him what it was like to hold a girl and kiss her like he does. Sometimes me and Twin One sneak around back of his house when my brother and his sister are together. Let me tell you, they do some heavy smooching."

"Has he ever caught you guys watching?" Mike asks.

"Yeah, once when she opened her eyes she saw us looking in the window and she ratted us out. By that time we'd seen enough already anyway," Tony says.

"Why did she have her eyes closed? Do you close your eyes when you and Patricia kiss?" Mike asks.

"I don't know, but sometimes I open my eyes to see if she's looking at me," Tony says as he thinks about it.

"Does she?" asks Mike.

"I'm not sure. I think we both open our eyes at the same time to see if we are looking at each other and then close our eyes again," Tony says. "Mike, you just have to try it for yourself. Practice in the mirror, close your eyes, and pucker your lips like you're kissing Jacquelyn."

"If I close my eyes, I won't be able to see."

"Man, you really need help. Open one eye so you can see."

Upset, Mike pulls his slingshot out of his hip pocket, picks up a pebble, and fires it in the direction of a tree in the yard. He misses.

Tony sits up straight, "Tell me you weren't trying to hit that tree."

"Maybe, why?" Mike asks.

Tony hits himself in the forehead with the palm of his hand, and then goes inside the house. After a while he comes out holding his Wham-O Sportsman Slingshot his brother bought him for his tenth birthday. "Let's go," he tells Mike, "it's time we break in your Wham-O."

"Where are we going?" Mike asks.

"Just follow me." They walk down the street and past the park to the train tracks. "There's enough ammo out here to fight off a herd of wild elephants. You see that sign over there?" Tony picks up a small stone and pulls back on the rubber band, and then lets it go. It hits the sign and makes a loud clanging sound.

"Do you think we should be using that sign as a target?" Mike asks nervously.

"You see anything else out here we can use?" Tony says.

"Not really," Mike replies.

For the rest of the day and the rest of the week Tony shows Mike how to shoot his slingshot. Mike can now boast that he can shoot a slingshot with accuracy.

"You really don't have to look hard for ammo around here. With all the oak trees you have all the acorns you can shoot. Just keep practicing and you'll never miss your target."

So whenever Mike can't leave the house, he loads up on acorns and puts his wooden target up against his father's garage in the backyard, and shoots his slingshot from his bedroom window. Mike hasn't seen Jacquelyn for a few days now, and he can't wait to see her and show off his slingshot. He is pretty confident using his slingshot, but can't get up the nerve to fight back. The day has come and can he see Jacquelyn, he puts his slingshot in his hip pocket with the intention of showing off his mad skills in front of her. On his way out the door, his mother sees the slingshot and tells him to march back to his room and put it up or she will take it.

"Mom, I'm not going to shoot it at anybody or nothing like that," says Mike. "I'm just going to the park and shooting it at an old trash can that blew over there last week."

She does not say anything to him, only stomps her feet and points at his room. Sadly, he returns to his room and puts the slingshot under his mattress and walks out to meet Jacquelyn and her friends at the park.

At the park, they swing on the swing. Mike is pushing Jacquelyn on the swing while they all talk when David and his friends walk up and start harassing the girls. He walks up to Mike and pushes him aside.

"Don't you have a toilet that needs cleaning?" Mike walks back and stands in front of David; they stare at each other for a moment. David's friends think it is funny and stand on either side of David with their arms folded. Mike believes it is better to ignore them and tries to look as stern as possible during the stare down. He tries to stand behind Jacquelyn as she sits on the swing, but David pushes him out from behind her again.

"She wants a real man to push her, not some skinny little goof like you," David says.

Jacquelyn jumps from the swing and says, "When you look in the mirror, I'm sure you don't see a man at all."

Mike gathers up the nerve to tell David to back off.

"Did you hear that, boys?" asks David.

"I didn't hear anything," they say, "maybe he needs to repeat it! The toilet boy got some kind of nerve." Then David stands chest to chest with Mike.

"Back off," Mike tells him through gritted teeth.

"Make me, toilet boy," David warns. He turns to look back at his two friends. Before Mike knows it, David turns and sucker-punches him in the stomach. A car goes by, blows the horn, and slows down.

"Let's go, David," his friends say. Mike is doubled over, holding his stomach when David grabs him by his shoulders and throws him to the ground. Then he runs off with his friends laughing. Jacquelyn and her friends stand watching Mike as he slowly gets up from his knees, and walk over to help him up and brush off the dirt from his clothes. Mike is trying not to let her see him cry, but Jacquelyn holds his face in her hands and kisses him on the lips and thanks him for standing up for her. She and her friends walk away in shock.

"I can't believe you did that!" Nancy says.

"I can't believe I did it either," Jacquelyn says in an excited tone. "I don't know why, but I just did."

"What was it like?" they ask her.

"A dream," she tells them as they walk home. Mike's stomach is still hurting, but he just had the most wonderful experience of his life.

"She kissed me on the lips," he says aloud. "Oh my God, she kissed me." He runs all the way over to Tony's house and tells him everything. Tony shakes him by the shoulders. "Was her body up against yours?" he asks.

Mike looks at him and says, "There are things that a man has to keep to himself."

Tony punches him in the arm and asks, "Are you going to see her again?"

"I sure hope so," Mike says with the biggest grin on his face.

"Man, your face is turning as red as that church hat Mrs. Walls wears."

"How many times do you think you've kissed Patricia?" Mike asks.

"Oh man, I lost count. When I told her I was going to try out for the football team she was all over me. We must have kissed for ten minutes."

"Ten minutes!" Mike shouts. "That's like a lifetime."

"That's when you know you're really kissing," Tony replies. "Hot chicks love athletes, and I'm going to be the hottest athlete at school."

"Yes, you and about a hundred others. You better hope Pat's dad don't find out about the two of you."

"Nah, he won't. It's her jealous sister you have to watch out for. She came home after a divorce and she's got all her things in the garage. Pat and I will be married forever and we're going to move from this old place and not worry about anybody here."

"I'm not sure if I'll ever leave here," Mike says.

Tony asks, "When you graduate, are you going to college?"

"Well that's what my parents want me to do," says Mike. Then he thinks for a second. "So I probably will have to leave here, huh?"

"Yep, you probably will if you want to go off to college. What about Jacquelyn?" Tony asks. "Does she have any plans for when she graduates?"

"I never asked her anything like that before," Mike replies.

"You might want to find out; there ain't anything here to stay for," Tony says with a frown. "I can't wait to leave this stinking place, and when I leave, I'm never coming back."

"Is it that bad?" Mike asks.

"I don't know anymore," Tony says. "All I know is I want to find a car and drive away from here and not look back."

"But you are doing so well here," protests Mike. "You don't have the problems like I have. Nobody picks on you or beats you up; they don't talk about your father like they do mine."

Tony just looks at Mike and shakes his head.

"I guess I just don't see why you are so anxious to leave." Mike's tone is a little lower.

"It ain't about what you can see, Mike. Not everything is as open as your life. There are things you can't see, and it's those things that people are trying to get away from."

"Yeah, I guess you're right," Mike says. "There are times all I can think about is running away, and then I think about how it would hurt my mother. Maybe that's why I'm not sure if I want to leave."

"Well Mike, you have to grow up, and when you do you have to decide what you want to do. My brothers are always helping me out. They give me advice and I listen. Two of my brothers just got back from the war, and all they talk about is going back to England and France, but when I asked Drew why he came back, he just looked at me weird and told me I ask too many questions. You kind of have to grow up in a hurry in this place. There ain't no time to be a boy long, you have to be a man to make it." Tony pauses and says, "When I look at your home I always say you have the perfect setup."

"And you don't?" Mike asks.

Tony leans back on the porch steps. He looks up, sighs, and says, "You don't know the half of it. Hey man, let's go over to your place for a while."

They walk back to Mike's house, where he asks his mother if it's okay to go to Sam's Drive-In for burgers and sodas.

"Sure it's okay," she says. "I want the two of you to stay out of trouble, you hear me?"

"Yes ma'am," they reply.

She goes to her room and comes out with two dollars, which she hands to Mike. They walk the hot trek to Sam's, sit down at a table the owner set out for those who walk up, and order their food.

"Just look at all the cool cars, Mike," says Tony. "Hey look, that's Mr. Silva's brother over there. He went to Dallas and came back with that new Chevrolet Fleet Master. Under the hood it comes with a 216 inline 6 cylinder engine. I don't know too much about engines right now, but I figure in a year or so there won't be a car made that I won't know what's under the hood. Right now all I can do is hope to get one someday before I'm an old man."

"We need to get a job, and we can both get what we want," says Mike.

"I went by there last week and talked to Old Man Silva to see if he would hire me, but he said that I should come back after I rebuild my first engine. Can you imagine that? How am I supposed to build an engine? You see one lying around, 'cause I sure don't. I was a little upset at first, but when I left his brother told me to come by on Saturday and he'll show me how to rebuild an engine. He said their pops told him the same thing, but his brother showed him how to rebuild an engine. He said his brother learned to rebuild when he was in the Army before the war broke out in Europe. They have an old Chevy engine out back of the shop he learned on, and he said he'll teach me on the same one. He said he ain't going to pay me to learn and most of it I'll have to learn on my own."

"What?" Mike says. "If you don't know about engines, how does he expect to you to learn on your own?"

"Well I asked the same thing when he said it. He pointed to a box of mixed tools and took me to the engine and told me, 'You do it by taking it apart and then putting it back together as many times as it takes until you know every part and what it does.'"

"So when do you start?"

"I start this Saturday. He said he'll give me the tools and I have to take it apart."

"I couldn't do that," Mike says. "That's crazy. What happens when you put it back together and you still have parts on the ground?"

"I asked him the same thing and he said I would have to take it all apart and put it back together again."

Mike puts his hands on his head and says, "That's nuts."

"It's only nuts if you don't have plans to leave. Pat and I already have plans to leave here, so I'm going to learn and do what I have to do to get out of here. That engine is my ticket out of RPSville," Tony says.

"What's that?" Mike asks.

Tony sits up straight and looks Mike stern in the face. "You of all people didn't just ask me that," he says. "RPS! Mike, everybody in this freaking town plays that dumb game all the time. It's like it's the only way they decide to do whatever it is they are going to do. Man Mike, I swear sometimes you're too smart for your own good." Then Tony pounds his right hand into his left hand, imitating the game.

Mike says, "Yeah, well when you are the subject of their stupidity you tend to be oblivious until they hit you. I notice when I hear it, and then I wait to see what happens next."

"I'll tell you this, Mike. When I have kids, I swear I don't ever want any of them playing that stupid game."

"Wow man, I've been saying the same thing for years." The carhop brings out their burgers, fries, and drinks. The boys pay for it and dig in.

"Man, Sam's makes the best burgers and fries in the world."

Tony holds up a finger as he tries to swallow what he has in his mouth. "I agree with all my burger."

After they eat, they start out walking to the tracks. Tony pulls his Wham-O out from under his shirt and Mike does the same. They find old cans and boxes to shoot at as they close their day. Mike and Jacquelyn haven't gone back to the park since David and his boys jumped on him, so they will meet up at the end of her street and walk to the drugstore together, where they enjoy an ice cream float together. The summer is coming to an end, and Mike's mother is busy at the school preparing for the start of the fall session. When he meets Jacquelyn at the corner he tells her that his mother is busy at the school, and she tells him that her mother is spending time at her grandmother's house. She is on her way to the grocer to get a few items for her mother. They walk to the store and she purchases the items her mother wants her to get, and then he walks her back to the house. On their way back he asks, "What are your plans after we graduate from high school?"

"I plan on going to college; I'm just not sure which one. What about you?" she asks.

"I plan on going to college also. My parents want me to try for Southwest Texas State Teachers College," he replies.

Jacquelyn screams and it scares Mike something fierce.

He stands in one place with his elbows locked to his side and his shoulders pushed up to cover his neck, looking for someone to walk out of nowhere and clobber the two of them.

"What did you do that for?" he demands.

"I'm so sorry," she says, "but when you said Southwest Texas State Teachers College, that's on the top of my list of colleges to attend."

"Oh my God, please warn a guy before you do that again. You nearly gave me a heart attack!"

"Please promise you'll try your best to get accepted there," she says.

He looks at her and says, "As long as you promise not to scream again."

"I promise, cross my heart." After that she walks home a little faster with the biggest smile on her face.

Chapter 5
Getting In Shape

Mike promises that he will do everything in his power not to cry this year when he gets picked on. Looking in the mirror, he whispers, "You've got to be the man Jacquelyn expects you to be."

Earlier he had another conversation with his father.

"Do not expect anything different at the high school level," his father said. "It may be different waters, but you'll find the same sharks. You have to outsmart and outwit them. They're not so brave when they act alone; that's why they are always there with their friends."

Mike thought, *Except Craig, he's a great white shark. He don't need friends when he's feeding on his victims.*

"They like to take the upper hand by being the first to throw the punch. Don't make it easy for them to hurt you — there are other ways to defend yourself. You have to learn to keep moving when they step in front of you; keep trying to go around them, and then if you can't get past them, give 'em a knuckle sandwich."

Mike laughed. His father never advocated violence before. "It sounds funny when you say that."

"I'm not saying you should get into a brawl or nothing like

that, but don't just stand in one place while they use you as a punching bag. Hit them back as hard as they hit you. Then if they beat you up, at least you can say you got a punch in."

They laughed at that. Mike takes his father's words to heart because he already knows that when David stands face to face with him, he looks around at his friends before turning quickly to punch him in the stomach.

The question Mike asks himself later while in bed is, *How do you avoid something like that? If I know that he's going to punch me when he turns around, do I punch him when his head is turned? What happens if I don't punch him hard enough?* "My head hurts," Mike says. Then he rolls over on his side and tries to sleep.

The next day Mike visits Tony.

Tony tells him, "Next week is school. Is everything going okay? You have to be ready by now — you've had your first kiss and now everybody in school will know that you and Jacquelyn are a thing. You can't tell me it doesn't get any better than that."

"I'm sure it can, but I'll just have to wait and see. I'm sure you already know that, right?" Mike says.

"You are right, my man. You are talking to the love expert. Patricia and I are inseparable. We are one, my man," Tony brags.

Mike laughs. "You should see yourself; you really need to stop. I think we need to change the subject."

"To what?" Tony asks.

Mike looks at Tony and says, "Cars, sports, anything but that, okay? Look, you said you wanted a car more than anything, but how are you going to buy one? Neither of us has a job to speak of; you spend every Saturday putting that engine thingy together and then tearing it down, and you can't buy cars with training."

"Yeah, but I can when I start working there. Old Man Silva has been watching me all summer and he's really impressed with my work. I must have torn that engine apart and rebuilt it ten times. He said that I picked it up faster than his brother. He wants me to come by Thursdays through Saturdays, and I can start with tune-ups and oil changes."

Mike grabs him by the shoulders and shakes him excitedly. "You got the job?"

"I got the job, my man," Tony says as he brushes back his hair.

"Congratulations! You said you'd do it and you did. I wish I were you..."

"No!" Tony stops him and sits up straight. Looking Mike in the eyes, he says, "Never wish you were someone else. You don't know what they're going through, so saying you want to be them is like saying you want the troubles and problems they have." Shaking his head and looking down, he continues, "Look Mike, I ain't told nobody this, so you better take this to your grave. You hear me?"

"Sure, yeah, Tony. What?"

Tony bites his lip. "I like my dad, but he's not always a good man to my mom and us; I'll say that and nothing more. Anyway I've told you too much already. I'm not telling you anything else. I shouldn't have told you that."

"Sorry," Mike says. "You know that I'll never tell anyone, right?"

"Yeah, we're cool," Tony tells him.

"Hey Tony, will you go to the grocer with me? Mr. Hardeman, the manager there, wanted to offer us a job. I didn't know that you got the job at Silva's Garage. Anyway, it's not much, but I will be stocking the shelves. He said that we have to be on time or he will can us."

"Thanks for looking out for me. When do you start?"

"I'm supposed to be there on Saturday; he's going to show me what I have to do." Sadly, Mike looks down at the ground. "Well, we have jobs now, so I guess we won't be able to hang out as much anymore."

"We still have school. And both our ladies are good friends so we'll still have time to hang out," Tony says.

Then Mike asks, "How much money do you think we have to save before we're able to afford a new car?"

"I'll ask Pops," says Tony. "He knows all about those things."

They leave Tony's home and start off toward the grocer. Mike talks to Mr. Hardeman and lets him know that he'll be the only one to come in. He shakes Mike's hand and tells him that he'll be expecting him promptly on Saturday for training.

Mike's freshman year goes as expected — only Craig is more interested in Susan Wells than he is in picking on him. He just wishes that David would lay off too. Every day after school Mike shows up at the grocer and makes sure all the shelves are stocked, and that the canned goods are facing forward and can be read without the customers having to turn them around to read the labels. Jacquelyn walks into the store and sees Mike cleaning the vegetable and fruit stands. When their eyes meet all they can do is smile at each other. At five foot six, Jacquelyn is wearing a beige poodle skirt with a blue plaid blouse, white bobby socks, and black penny loafers; her hair is dark brown and she wears it in a white crochet snood.

Mike breaks the silence and says, "You know this is where my dad and mom met."

"Really?" she says as she walks toward him, looking at the cans and sweeping her finger along the front edge of the shelf.

"Yes! Right at the checkout, he told me." Mike thinks to himself, *She looks like the most beautiful angel I have ever seen.* "Wow uh… what brings you here?" he asks, snapping out of his trance.

"The fruit," says Jacquelyn. "My mother wants to make a fruit salad to go with dinner tonight." She walks up to him and rubs her arm against his. "What do you suggest?" She picks up an apple and holds it up close to her face, and then turns slightly to meet his eyes. "Which one of these apples do you recommend?"

Swallowing, he gasps, "Well I would suggest these. I just put those out. The others have been out most of the day, and most of those have bruises."

She gathers three of them and walks away slowly. Looking back and smiling, she says, "Why, I thank you kindly, sir." Then she walks away with the apples and grapes as Mike looks on. When she is finally out of his sight, he can't believe his luck. Holding his hands to his side, he turns around, bends over, and in a quite tone yells, "Yes!" Some of the women look at him and smile, but one woman in the aisle pompously holds her head up and snarls, "I never" as she walks away. Mike is too excited to let that taint the moment.

Time passes and now Mike and his friends are juniors, and he's not being harassed as much as in previous years. He quit the grocer and started working at the soda fountain for Doc Jacobs at the drugstore. That way in his free time he can make the best ice cream floats for Jacquelyn when she stops by to see him.

One morning after he and Jacquelyn leave the school cafeteria, they walk to the stands and talk until it's time for class. Walking across the parking lot, he hears the game being played behind him; he can hear Wesley and Ronald beginning the game: "Rock, Paper, Scissors," He hears. David is walking in front of him while Wesley and Ronald walk behind him, getting ready to pull his pants down. It's been three years, and Mike has changed the way he combs his hair and wears his pants; he tries to defend himself as much as he is able to. At sixteen going on seventeen, he is six feet tall; he has red hair and weighs one hundred thirty pounds soaking wet, and is still the skinniest boy in the school. His parents have him keep his hair cut short because they worried he was trying to join a gang when he tried to grow it long.

When Mike hears the boys finish their game he turns to face them. "Just kidding," they say. And just then David, who is walking in front of them, waits until they turn their backs and then grabs both sides of Mike's pants and yanks down as hard as he can; he pulls Mike's pants down to his knees. The school grounds erupt in a roar of laughter. Being used to all the boys' pranks, he bends down and pulls his pants up in a calm manner, and then he turns to see David laughing, walking backwards with his hands up. Tony is standing behind David, waiting for him to walk into him. He hands his books to Patricia, and when David gets close enough to him he grabs his pants on both sides of his hips and pulls down as hard as he can, right down to

David's ankles. Unbalanced, David turns around to see who did it and swings at the same time, only to be pushed to the ground with his feet and pants above his body. Struggling to get his pants back on from the ground, he gets up and runs through the laughing crowd of students. Tony, now sixteen years old going on seventeen at five foot eleven inches tall, with thick black hair and a well-built one hundred seventy-pound body, is still laughing; he walks over to Mike and Jacquelyn.

"He'll remember to wear underpants the next time he comes to school. By the way, that's pretty clever wearing your gym shorts under your pants, man. I'll have to remember that next time," Tony says, admiring Mike's ingenuity.

"Yes," says Mike. "I wear my belt a little loose so when they do it, my gym shorts will still be up."

Jacquelyn protests, "If you little boys would grow up and stop playing these silly pranks on each other, that wouldn't be necessary, now would it?"

"Well Miss Westbury," says Tony, "boys will be boys." The four of them continue on across the parking lot to the door going into the school, talking about the coming summer and the new 1949 cars that came out a few months earlier. Tony tells them that he has his eyes on a 1935 Chevrolet four-door sedan.

"My pop told me that if I can fix it, I can have it."

"What do you mean by 'fix it'?" asks Jacquelyn.

"Well it's in Old Man Danby's garage with a busted engine," says Tony, pulling up on his shirt collar, "but I want you to know there ain't no engine made that I can't fix. Mr. Danby wants seventy dollars for it. He told my pops that he wants it out of the garage by next week or he will send it to the junk heap. His wife must be really nagging him about not being able to park her new 1948 Plymouth two-door Coupe in the garage. I've worked two years to get me a car and now I'll have it by Saturday. The body is clean and the tires are okay, and when I get that car in pop's garage, me and the boys will start rebuilding the engine the same day. Man, I can't wait. I can totally rebuild that engine and be rolling in a week."

"Yeah, you've had a lot of practice," says Mike. "Me myself, I can only dream of getting a car. I don't think I'll be driving anytime soon; I haven't earned enough money to get a car on my own and my parents can't afford to help me buy one. I quit the grocer because Mr. Hardeman cut my hours and I was barely making enough to buy a bike, let alone a car, and I'm not making much more working the fountain at the drugstore, but at least I work five days a week."

"I'll tell you what," Tony says, "if I find another sweet deal like I got, you buy the car and I'll rebuild it for you."

Mike smiles real big and Jacquelyn tells him, "That would be a really nice thing for you to do."

The boys walk the girls to their class, and then turn around and head off for the gym. When they arrive at the gym, David is still fuming and threatening to get both Tony and Mike back for what they did to him in the parking lot. Craig, now eighteen going on nineteen years of age, at six foot four and weighing over two hundred fifty pounds, is a menacing figure around the school; he walks up to David, leans against the wall with his hand, and shoves his face in David's face.

"You and your little clowns should grow up and put an end to the pranks." He points in David's face and then grabs him by the neck.

"Tony is on the varsity football and track teams, and if you do anything to jeopardize their chances of winning, then you and those clown friends of yours will have to deal with me."

"Sure Craig," David says nervously, gasping for air.

"You better understand where I'm coming from. If I lose money because you and your friends are too stupid to understand, then I promise I won't be the only one losing something." Craig lets him go when one of the guys lets him know the coach just walked in the door.

"Sure Craig, I understand. You know me; I'm just blowing off a little steam, that's all. We're cool, Craig. Have I ever let you down before?" asks David, fearing for his life.

Craig walks away and looks back at him. "By the way, I don't know when you stopped wearing drawers and I don't care, but you better start wearing some soon. Nobody rides in my car without drawers unless you're one of the ladies, and you ain't no lady."

The guys laugh as they walk out of the gym dressing room. David leans back and looks at everybody who is staring at him. Angry, he curses and yells at everyone in the gym. Coach Grey, who's as big as a side of beef and an inch taller than Craig, walks up to David, who's five foot nine inches tall and weighs one hundred thirty pounds; he grabs him by the back of his collar and walks him out of the dressing room. Then Coach Grey takes him out of the gym and tosses him out and tells him he is never to come back.

Still cursing, David grabs a pack of cigarettes from the sleeve of his shirt and lights one, then leaves the school campus swearing that he will get all of them back.

"I'll get you bastards, just wait and see. I'll get all of ya if it is the last thing I do. And if Craig thinks he can embarrass me like that in front of the guys again, he'll have another thing coming."

Coach Grey walks back into the gym and yells at everybody, "hurry up, get dressed, and be out on the field in ten minutes." Tony and the other students hurry to get dressed, and are still talking about David while jogging out to the track. Mike jogs out with the others while they run warm-up laps around the track. He is doing his best to keep up with them, but only manages to run a single lap before cramping up and finding it hard to breathe. He stops on the side of the track to throw up. The girls who are watching are grossed out by his actions. One of the runners walks up to him and tells him he shouldn't start off running that hard or he'll kill himself. He hands him a cup of water and a salt tablet.

"You take this and you'll feel better," he says. "Then when you're ready to run, start slow before trying to do more."

Mike sits on the ground admiring all the athletes on the track. When he feels better, he gets up and back on the track as Coach Grey calls him over.

"I saw you running a bit ago," he says. "How are you feeling?"

"Oh, I'm okay now, coach. I just got a little overheated, but now I'm ready to start again."

"Well hold your horses, son; I don't think you're ready for sports yet," says Coach Grey.

"I am, coach. I promise. I've been working really hard at it."

"I'll tell you what, we'll play a game of Rock, Paper, Scissors. You win, you're on the team; you lose and I want you off my track."

"You're joking, right, coach?"

"You ever see me joke, boy?"

"No sir," Mike answers.

"Get your hands up and let's start... Rock, Paper, Scissors." In the middle of Coach Grey's swing down, he half opens his hand and gives Mike the impression that he is going with paper, so Mike chooses scissors and Coach Grey drops rock.

"Rock crushes scissors, son. Say goodnight to the girls, and on your way out, get the hose and clean that mess off my track."

Mike looks back at him as he jogs off the track and tells him, "Get it yourself." He runs into the gym thinking of what he was told: *Start slow, and then try to do more after that.* He figures that he will start by jogging after school, if he has the time after walking Jacquelyn home. He sits on the bench in the dressing room and pulls off his gym clothes. He wonders what it would be like if he were an all-star athlete like his friends. He sits there crying because he thinks of himself as always being such a weak jerk. Someone walks in and Mike quickly wipes the tears from his face and finishes changing his clothes. Then he walks over to the water fountain, takes a swallow of water, and makes his way back to the bleachers to watch his friends warm up on the track before they practice for the next track meet. He thinks, *Next year I'll be ready to run and I will make the track team; all I have to do is run faster than Joey Kemp, and then Coach Grey and Coach Webb will have to let me on the team. Joey is the slowest person on the team, so if I can outrun him it would be one of the proudest moments of my entire life.*

After school Tony drives the girls to the drive-in theater and then he and Mike go to work themselves. Mike expresses that he wants to learn to run track.

"I really want to run, but Coach Grey doesn't want me on the team. Maybe next year I will be ready, and then I believe I can make the team."

"Well," Tony says, "I really don't have time to teach you. You kind of have to be a natural; otherwise you have to practice every day."

"I think I can do that. I'll run to the school and then run on the track and back home every day if I have to."

"Mike, you're a good guy, but I wouldn't want you to kill yourself trying to impress Jacquelyn. Man, she really likes you the way you are." Tired, Tony sighs and waves him off. "I have to get to Old Man Silva's before he starts screaming at me for being late."

Mike acknowledges him and asks if he could drop him off at the corner so that he can go home and change shirts. He gets out of the car and waits until Tony drives off; then he runs to the next block down the street from the park before going home.

"Hello Mother, I'm not going to eat right now so I won't be late for work at the drugstore. Doc Jacobs depends on me to be prompt to work at the soda fountain."

"Well Doc Jacobs can wait; you're going to sit down and eat."

"Mom, I have to change clothes," says Mike, "and I don't want Doc Jacobs to get on me for being late. I'll grab a bite on my way out."

"Okay," she says, "don't forget my prescription before you leave work. Your father already paid for it."

As he walks toward the door, she hands him a note as a reminder so that he doesn't forget. He sighs and then he runs all the way to work. When he gets off work he puts his mother's prescription in his pocket and runs all the way home. Mike does this for the rest of the school year; during the summer, in the fall, and in the winter he gets his body in shape for track season. And no matter how hard he tries, he is still not allowed to participate in any of the sports. Disappointed because of all the running he's done, Mike just shrugs it off and continues to run almost everywhere he goes. He likes the way he feels and knows in his heart he is in better shape than Joey Kemp.

Chapter 6
Renewed Spirit

Mike's senior year has been a lot less eventful than other years. He's finally becoming a man who will soon be making his own decisions in life, and he can't wait to leave all of his troubles behind. This is the big night that everyone has been waiting for; he and his friends are all excited about the days ahead.

"Good morning, Mother. Has Father already left for work?"

"Yes, he had to be at the school early this morning; he has a lot of setting up to do at the elementary school library for the PTA meeting tomorrow night. Most of the women in town will be there, and as a favored teacher" — she smiles and turns to do a curtsy — "I have the responsibility of giving the welcome speech, so I will be a little late. I've already told your father that he'll have to warm up his food, so I'm going to leave your food in the ice box with your father's."

"Mother, that's what I'm trying to tell you," Mike says. "I may be home late also. The big game is tomorrow night, remember? Tonight everybody will be at the drive-in for the movie *Twelve O'Clock High*, and tomorrow is the big game, and everybody will be there; then there's the sock hop Saturday in the school gym."

"Are you and Jacquelyn going together?" she turns and asks.

"Yes Mother, and yes, we'll be riding with Tony and Patricia. Doc Jacobs told me I can close the soda fountain at five o'clock so I'll have time to come home and change shirts, and then go to the movie tonight, and I'll be able to make it to the game tomorrow."

She walks over to him and fixes his tie. "You mind your manners, you hear?"

"Yes Mother, I always do," he says.

After school, Tony drops Patricia and Jacquelyn off at the drive-in theater for work, and then he drops Mike off at the drugstore before going to Silva's Garage. "I'll walk over to the garage after I close the fountain, and then we can go to the drive-in when you get off work."

"That's the plan. Mr. Silva's wife is not feeling so good these days, so his brother is watching the garage. Whenever he's in charge, he lets me go early. I told him we were going to see the movie *Twelve O'Clock High* tonight at the drive-in, and he said that he and his girlfriend would be there too, so I don't plan on being there too late tonight."

"Great, then I'll see you when I get there." He walks into the empty drugstore, where Doc Jacobs is waiting for him to run the soda fountain.

"Good afternoon, Doc," Mike says.

"Afternoon Mike, glad to see you; it finally got quiet in here, so I'll be in the back if you need me."

"Okay," Mike says. "I'll go ahead and clean under the counter and sweep the floor."

Doc Jacobs walks away and gives him a thumbs-up. Mike is wiping the counter off when Craig and Susan Wells walk in. She goes over and rings the bell, and when Doc Jacobs walks up to the counter she hands him a prescription for her mother. Then she turns and walks over to the soda fountain to join Craig, who has already chugged down one Coke and ordered a second one.

"Hey Mike," Susan greets him.

"Hello Susan, can I get you a soda?" Mike asks.

"Sure, why not?" she replies.

He fills the glass and sets it on the counter for her. Then Mr. Baines walks in looking for Doc Jacobs. "He's in the back," Mike tells him. "Just ring the bell."

Before he can ring the bell, Doc Jacobs walks up to the counter.

"How can I help you, Mr. Baines?"

"Oh, I need this prescription filled, thank you."

"How's your leg?" Doc Jacobs asks.

"Not much better," says Mr. Baines. "They told me to stay off it for a while."

"You should," Doc says. "Walking around on it will only make it worse."

"Yeah, I know." Jokingly, Mr. Baines adds, "As soon as I get this prescription filled I'm going straight home and I'm going to sleep until next week."

"All right, well, let me get this so you can get on home. Take a seat there and take the load off." Doc walks to the back to fill the prescriptions he has stacking up.

Mrs. Walker comes in to get her prescription filled, and her husband goes to the soda fountain for a glass of Coke. Doc takes her prescription to the back with the prescription for Mr. Baines.

Doc Jacobs calls Mike to the back. "Ring this up for Susan for me," he says.

"Sure thing, Doc," says Mike.

When he walks out he calls Susan over to the counter to ring up her purchase. After he finishes, Craig walks out the door with Susan, without paying for the three sodas they had. Mike walks around the counter and out of the store behind them, and tells Craig that he has to pay for the sodas. Craig and Susan ignore him and get into the car. From the car Craig tells Mike, "If I lose, I will pay for the sodas. And if I win you pick up the tab." Before they start the game, Mike takes a deep breath and looks up at the sky; then he backs away from the car. Craig and Susan start the game of Rock, Paper, Scissors… Mike already knows what the result will be, so he takes another step back and Craig yells, "Scissors cut paper! Looks like you pick up the tab, soda jerk." Then he drives off laughing as Mike watches in anger, shaking his fist at him.

"One day you'll wish you never played that stupid game with me, Craig. One day, you jackass." He turns and walks back into the store as Mr. Baines is walking out.

"You have a good night, sir," Mike says with a frown on his face.

"And you do the same, young man."

Mr. Walker finishes his soda, but Mrs. Walker is still waiting for her prescription to be filled, so her husband orders a second one. After a couple of hours, things slow down at both the drugstore and the soda fountain.

"You can close the fountain now, Mike," Doc calls out.

"Yes sir, Doc. I was about to do just that." After cleaning the fountain and sweeping the floor, Mike lets Doc Jacobs know he is finished and leaving. He closes the door, walks down to the garage, and waits for Tony to end his night.

At the drive-in Tony finds a good spot to park in the middle so that they can have the best view in front of the screen. He and Mike go inside and walk up to the counter for soda and popcorn. Patricia nudges Jacquelyn to let her know the boys are at the counter. Jacquelyn looks over her shoulder and blows a kiss at Mike. Tony punches him in the arm, and then grabs him in a headlock. "Man, I want to see what you look like after ten years of marriage. You do know she's going to want you to marry her and have like ten kids, right?"

Mike just stands there with the biggest grin on his face. Combing his hair, he asks, "What about you and Pat? You guys going to tie the knot or what?"

"Oh yeah, man, and we're going to have at least five boys."

Craig and David are at the other end of the counter harassing the girls inside. David sees Mike and Tony at the other end of the counter, and then chews a small wad of paper, pushes it into a straw, and blows it out; he hits Jacquelyn on her butt and laughs. Craig stares Mike down as if to say "come on over; I'll punch your lights out if you're man enough." Tony is holding Mike back.

"They're not worth it, man."

Craig and David get their hot dogs, drinks, and popcorn for themselves and their dates, and head back to the car. Before David walks out, he flips Mike and Tony the finger while carrying his box of food. Tony brushes his hair back, gives David the finger, and then turns to see him face to face; he tells him without speaking "any time," and pounds his fist into his hand. Jacquelyn and Pat finish serving the other guests and walk over to the counter to get Mike and Tony's order.

"Hey gorgeous," Tony greets Pat. Then she checks to see if her boss is looking her way and leans over the counter to kiss Tony. Jacquelyn and Mike look on, and he grabs her hand and squeezes it. She smiles at him, while he blushes and winks at her. They talk for as long as they can, and then hurry to get the boys a hot dog, Coke, and popcorn. The boys pay for their order, and then Pat looks over her shoulder again and sees that her boss is not looking before she jumps up on the counter to give Tony a big hug and kiss. Jacquelyn tells Mike that she will see him when the movie is over and her shift ends.

"Okay," Mike says. "Until then."

The boys walk out to the car to watch the movie.

After the movie they close the drive-in. Tony and Mike wait outside, sitting on the trunk of the car until the girls finish their shift. When they walk up, Pat throws her sweater over her shoulder and leans against the car, while Mike and Jacquelyn climb into the backseat and wait for Tony and Pat to finish smooching.

The next day the whole school is abuzz with excitement and looking forward to the game, and all the talk is about who's bringing whom to the sock hop Saturday night. Tony tells Mike that he has the night off because of the game, and then asks, "Will you walk the girls to the game, and after I'll drive us home?"

"Sure Tony, I'll do that just like all the games we have at the school."

Mike closes the fountain early, and is waiting when Jacquelyn and Pat walk in, ready to go the game. The air is electric and they are all excited because it is their homecoming game, and the buzz is the fact that they are seniors and there is only this year between them and adulthood. The walk to the school passes quickly because of the conversation, and all the homecoming mums the girls made, and the thought of life after high school. When they get to the game they see Craig and Susan in the stands, and David by the field on the far end. They get a seat in the stands between a group of adults and call out to Tony when he is not in the game. The homecoming parade is the highlight when Danielle Summers is crowned Homecoming Queen and Nathan Edwards is crowned Homecoming King. The game goes great and they win 13 to 6.

After the excitement of the night is over, they wait for Tony to get dressed and then they all leave for Sam's Drive-In. The boys pick up the tab; the night could not have ended any better. They talk for most of the night and decide that they will go to the sock hop at six o'clock on Saturday. Mike and Tony will go to work in the morning, and hope to be finished by three o'clock. Tony will go home and bathe, change, and then pick up Mike at his house around five o'clock. They will have time to drop by the girls' houses and pick them up before the dance.

Saturday afternoon Mike lets Tony know that he has to work late and that he is to go ahead and pick the girls up, and he will meet them at the gym. Jacquelyn tells him that she will wait on Mike to get off work and they will walk to the gym together, and Pat and Tony will meet them there. After the confusion of words, Tony lets them know that he will be glad to take them home after the dance.

Mike thinks for sure that either Craig or David will be looking for him after the stare down at the drive-in. He is nervous, and will do everything he can to avoid them and those who follow them. Mike stops by the grocer while on break at the same time David walks up behind him outside the store and grabs him, pushing him into the wall with his face pressed against it. James, David's younger brother, walks by and puts his hand on the wall next to Mike's face.

"All you have to do is say 'uncle' and David will let you go."

"Okay," he struggles. "Uncle."

"I can't hear you, toilet breath," says David.

"UNCLE!" he shouts.

David, laughing, gives Mike one last shove into the wall. Then he walks away with his friends.

"Sorry about that," James apologizes, "I don't know what's gotten into him these days."

Mike looks at him and says, "You could have gotten him off me."

"He's my brother... besides, it didn't hurt to say 'uncle.' It's a lot better than a couple of punches in the back, don't you think?"

"I guess," Mike says. "Thanks." Mike walks away and goes into the store angry. He walks to the fruit stand and crushes a couple oranges and a grapefruit, leaving them in the stand.

James feels bad for what just happened and thinks it would be better to follow Mike in case David tries to act out his aggression again. If he does, James thinks he will intercede and stop him before things get out of hand. He walks up to the fruit stand and picks out the crushed fruit and then throwing them away.

Mike stops by Silva's Garage and talks to Tony while he is taking a break. He talks about the dance. "Tony... Can you dance?"

"Man, me and Pat have been practicing the Jitterbug, the Charleston, and other swing dances. I hope you're not here for dance lessons, 'cause it ain't happening, man."

Mike laughs. "No, Jacquelyn and I have been trying those and something called the Lindy Hop. Have you heard of it?"

"Yeah man, that's almost the same as the Jitterbug. My mom's taught me that one."

"I don't know if I can dance in front of people. Jacquelyn teaching me is one thing, but not with a crowd of people," Mike explains.

Tony laughs. "Man, if she taught you any of the slow dances, just do that. Act like the two of you are the only people in the gym. I'll see you later, man, I have to get back to work so I can leave in a couple of hours."

"Yeah, I had better be going myself." Mike hurries back to the drugstore without going home to drop off the canned goods from the grocer so that he can get his time in and hope to close before six that night. With most of the school preparing for the sock hop, he hopes that no one will bother to come into the drugstore. At five o'clock, Tony and the girls show up to find a frustrated Mike still tending the soda fountain, with three people waiting in line for their prescriptions to be filled.

"Hey man, you still slaving over the soda fountain?"

"Yeah," he replies. "Of all the days, we would be the busiest today. Look," Mike continues, "you guys go ahead and I'll meet you there. I'm going to get a head start on cleaning, and if anybody else comes in, I'm going to tell them we are out of

Coke and it'll be Monday before we get more in. It won't be the first time we've run out, so they'll understand. I'll shut down at six sharp and I'll be at the gym no later than six thirty."

"Well, I'll hold a sign up and let all the boys know that my dances are reserved for you only, so don't be late," Jacquelyn tells Mike.

"I'm looking forward to it," he replies. They smile at each other and Pat pushes Jacquelyn. "Go ahead and kiss him, girl. If you're waiting on him, you'll be an old maid before he puckers his lip."

Tony mocks him and says, "That's because his lips will be puckered from old age."

They laugh and Mike punches Tony in the arm as they leave the drugstore. Before Jacquelyn walks out the door, she turns and blows Mike a kiss.

"That's for the man in my life."

They get into the car, and Tony backs out of the parking lot and heads out down Main Street. Mike watches Jacquelyn watching him from the back window. He sighs and wishes he were in the car with her.

At five forty-five Mike tells Doc that he has finished with all the cleaning and asks if it's okay to cut out a little early.

"Sure," Doc tells him, "get out of here and enjoy the dance."

Mike thanks him and tells him that he will. He runs home and changes clothes. Of course his mother inspects his attire and briefs him on carrying himself like the gentleman she expects him to be.

"Okay, Mother. I'll behave myself. I'm late and I have to be going now, please." He kisses her and then walks out the door. He runs to the main highway on his way to the school. Craig sees him and pulls up in his car. Susan opens the door and tells him to hurry up. He hesitates but runs up to the door anyway, and Craig pulls off, spinning his tires in the gravel and showering Mike with rocks and dust. Mike curses in anger as he watches them drive down the road laughing. Then he looks down and tries to dust himself off. He kicks the rocks and yells that he will get Craig and get him where it costs him the most.

When Mike arrives at the gym, Jacquelyn asks why he is so dirty. He tells her what Craig and Susan did, including not paying for their sodas a couple days before.

"That's behind me now," he says. "And now I'm here for my dance."

All night they dance together, enjoying the moment, especially when they have the chance to dance close.

"We're seniors now, and we have to make plans for when we graduate from college," she says.

"Whoa," Mike says, "I was thinking of when we graduate in a few months from high school."

"You have to start thinking long-term now, Michael," Jacquelyn tells him. "If you are going to be the man of the house, you have to look forward to our wedding, and our children..."

"Hold on now; let me age gradually," he says, holding his hands on top of his head. "Besides Jacquelyn, you're going to Southwest Texas State Teachers College, and I haven't even heard from them yet."

"Oh yes," she pulls him off the dance floor and over to the table where Tony and Pat are sitting. "Sit down and close your eyes." She reaches into her purse with her back to him and looks over her shoulder. Telling him not to peek, she sets an envelope on the table and says, "Okay, you can open your eyes." Mike looks down at the envelope and picks it up. When he looks at the letterhead, he sees it is from Southwest Texas State Teachers College.

"Open it," Tony tells him.

"Okay," he says with a big grin on his face. He opens the letter, and with a sigh and disappointment on his face, he tosses it on the table and gets up to walk off. Jacquelyn grabs the letter and reads it.

"What?" she says in surprise. "You've been accepted!"

He turns around laughing. "Got you!"

She gets up from the table, jumps into Mike's arms, and kisses him for the first time in public. The whole crowd around them woos and claps. She holds his letter of acceptance and tells everyone that they are going to Southwest Texas State Teachers College together. Craig, whose teachers have been passing him along through his grades just to get him out of the school system, is angry. He walks over, separates them, pushes Mike to the floor, and grabs the letter from Jacquelyn, ripping it up and throwing it on Mike's chest as he stares down at him, daring him to get up and do something. Coach Webb pushes through the crowd with Coach Grey close behind him, and they tell Craig to report to the office on Monday. "We'll talk about your behavior then. In the meantime, break it up and go back over to Susan where you belong."

Craig walks away and pushes past Tony, who is standing slightly in front of him to keep him off Mike. Tony helps Mike up off the floor, and they walk back over to the table. After about thirty minutes, things settle down a bit. They decide to leave and head to Sam's Drive-In Café to order food.

"Well," Mike says, "in a few months we'll graduate, and Jacquelyn and I will be going down to San Marcos. There will be no Craig or his puppet minion David." They eat their burgers, fries, and malted drinks, and give a toast to their future.

Chapter 7
Final Conflict

Mike and Tony are sitting in the car talking about their future. Tony tells him that he has enlisted in the Army, and that he'll be leaving the next month for boot camp at Fort Sill.

"I'll be training as a helicopter mechanic. Man, I can't wait to see those great flying machines. I'll try to keep in touch with you and Jacquelyn. I want to be the godfather of all ten of your kids."

They laugh for a while, and then Mike tells him that he is really looking forward to college.

"You will have to write us to let us know when you are graduating from boot camp. I really can't see you with all your hair cut off — shaved clean, man. In the movies, you can see that after you finish boot camp they let you grow it back."

"Yeah, I sure hope so because Pat really likes to rub her hands through my hair," says Tony. "Nothing like rubbing your hands through a head full of thorns." He sighs and turns his head to look out the driver's side window.

"What's wrong?" Mike asks.

"All my life I wanted to leave this place, and now that we are ready to leave… I'm not sure if I'll miss this place or not."

"Yes, I know the feeling," Mike says. "We've been talking about leaving all these years, and now here we are. And we are finding it hard to leave!"

"When you graduate from high school you're expected to leave home, but some people move back. I'm not sure if I want to do that. I want to make my home as far away from here as possible."

"Well, Jacquelyn and I will still be here in Texas, but it's big enough so that when we leave, it will feel like we are in another state," Mike says.

"By the way, Mike, Pat and I want you and Jacquelyn to be at our wedding. We are getting hitched next week before I leave. Pat already told Jacquelyn, but she wants me to tell you that she's pregnant."

"What?" Mike asks in surprise. He punches Tony in the arm. "Wow, I guess you're getting an early start on those boys. What do you know about that?" Excitedly, Mike continues. "Hot damn, congratulations man. So where's the wedding going to be?"

"Well it's going to be at the courthouse, but it will just be us guys. No one knows that she's pregnant, but they all know that I'm leaving for the Army in a month."

"We'll be there for you guys. I'm working late today, so I'll meet you at Sam's Drive-In Café tonight, and we'll all get together and talk about how many boys you'll have."

That evening, before Mike leaves the store, he thinks it might be good if he grabs his little friend when he gets home. He is not sure if he will use it if Craig pulls the same stunt he did before.

Mike walks to Sam's Drive-In Café to meet up with Tony and the girls. He goes home first and pulls out his slingshot, thinking he can protect himself from Craig and David, and then run for his life after he's shot both of them with rocks. When he arrives at the café, Tony's car is not there, so he waits for them for half an hour. Craig and David show up without their girls, and as usual they harass the carhops. Mike thinks it would be best to sneak off since Tony and the girls have not shown up yet. He starts off on the road looking for them, thinking that if they come his way, they would see him and they could pick him up from there. Walking on the side of the road at night is a little scary; it worries him because of the cars rushing by from behind. So Mike thinks it is better to walk on the other side, even with their lights on, although it would be hard to recognize Tony's car if they pass by. Then he thinks of what Craig and Susan did when he was walking to the sock hop, and he picks up the biggest palm-sized rock that his slingshot can shoot. Placing it in his pocket, he picks up a couple more rocks off the side of the street to take practice shots. Satisfied, Mike knows those two jackasses will pass his way, so he is prepared just in case Tony and the girls are delayed. He hears a truck rumbling up behind him, and then the sound of Craig burning rubber and blowing his horn like he always does when he leaves the drive-in. Since he is on the opposite side of the street, he would have a hard time hitting Craig's car, especially since he is speeding, so Mike hides in the cornfield while the truck goes by. Suddenly, Craig goes speeding by; he is already driving on the wrong side of the street to pass the truck — on the same side he is hiding.

Crazy luck, Mike thinks. *This is my chance.* He can see David waving his hand, rooting Craig on. Mike pulls back on the sling and lets it go from the cover of the cornfield. The sound of the rock hitting the front grill of Craig's Chrysler is really loud, and Mike thinks Craig will lose control of the car for sure when he hears it. The rock passes through Craig's grill, but he can't stop because he is passing the truck and a car is coming head on, so he guns it and runs the other car off the road. Red lights pull out from the other side of the road, and sirens sound as they chase Craig down the highway. Mike jumps up and down as he sees the police in pursuit of Craig. He knows that he buried that rock into Craig's grill for sure. Feeling good, he walks a little farther and crosses the street in all the excitement, high-stepping and waving his arms in the air. At that time, Tony and the girls see him walking from the café and think he is waving at them, and then they turn around to pick him up. After he gets into the car, Tony tells him that Pat is a little sick and that is why they are late. He also says that she really doesn't want to go to the drive-in to eat tonight.

"Oh, that's okay. We can just hang out somewhere. Let's go to the store and get a couple of sodas." Jacquelyn looks at him and says, "You're behaving a little strange."

"Am I?" asks Mike.

She points at him but says nothing else. She keeps her eyes on him the whole ride to the store.

When they drive up to the store, Craig and the police officer are standing in front of his car looking at the grill. The officer has finished writing the ticket for Craig's speeding. Tony and Mike go into the store and get the sodas. Jacquelyn notices the slingshot under Mike's shirt, and he pulls his shirt down over it when he climbs out of the backseat. After getting their sodas, they walk over to Craig's car, which has drawn a crowd. Craig has the hood up with a hole in the grill, and water leaking from the radiator. He is using a metal bar to pry the rock out from his grill. The officer tells him that he will give him a push with the cruiser across the street to Silva's Garage.

Tony walks up to the car, notices the damage, and says, "Old Man Silva probably wouldn't be able to get to it for another week. He's really tied up right now."

Craig looks up at Mike and shouts, "What are you looking at?"

Mike turns and walks away, just waving his Coke bottle at Craig. Then he mumbles, "Rock, Paper, Scissors, you ignorant bastard." And then he and Tony get back into the car.

The girls ask, "What's going on over there?"

Tony says, "Craig is getting another ticket for speeding, and he has a large rock in his radiator... it looks like he'll be needing a new one."

Jacquelyn looks at Mike with a smile, sits back in her seat, takes a swallow of his Coke, and whispers to herself. "Good for Mike. Good for you." Then they leave and drive off to their hangout spot overlooking the drive-in theater.

Chapter 8
Blurred Lines

Tapping on the window startles him. Wiping his eyes, Mike sits and wonders how long he has been there. He is not sure if he had fallen asleep or simply relived his entire childhood. He looks down at his hands and out the window to see what pulled him out of his past. His vision is blurred and he can't recognize the figure standing at his door, so he rolls down the window and looks up at a woman he thinks he might recognize.

"You wouldn't happen to be Michael Oliver James III, would you?" she asks.

"Yes I am, and do I have the pleasure of meeting Patricia Ann Reams?" he asks.

"The same," she replies.

"Give me a minute, please," says Mike. "I don't move as fast as I used to." Blinking his eyes to correct his vision and collect his thoughts, he rolls the window up and turns the engine off. He steps out of the car as the time between times fades. He looks around at all the cars that fill the parking lot as he gives her a big hug.

"It's been a long time," he says "Just wait until Jackie hears about this!"

"Twenty-five years," she replies.

"I guess we lost touch with you guys in '75 when you went to Germany. Not sure where you moved to after that."

"Right. I knew that you and Jacquelyn were moving, but we didn't have your new address," she says. "Oh, you don't know how disheartening that was for me. I must have cried for a week."

"Well, we can't get that time back, but we can have a new start," Mike says, comforting her.

He looks for Tony and asks, "Is Tony already in the gym? I must have dozed off for a minute waiting for everyone to show up."

"No, Tony didn't make this trip," she tells him.

"I did remember him saying once he graduated from school he would never return."

"Actually, he returned a few times, but it was to come and get me and the kids, and while he was here he visited his parents."

They stand there and talk for a little while about Tony.

Pat brings Mike up on the past fifty years. "After Tony joined the Army they sent him to Korea, and he stayed there in that war until '53. As you know, I stayed here with Tony Jr. and waited for Sr. to come home from the war and get us. We moved to Fort Stewart in Georgia and lived there until 1960. Jackie and I were still in communication with each other back then, and Tony continued to advance in his Army career. In 1960 we were transferred to Camp Pieri in Wiesbaden, Germany. We had five children then, three boys and two girls, with one on the way."

"Wow! That must have been a hard time for you trying to get five kids in line and moving in the same direction."

"Yes it was," she agrees. "It took me a while to get used to it, but you soldier on, as we say. In 1968 Tony started his first tour in Vietnam, where he served three tours until 1973. While he was there the kids and I moved from Germany back here to Thumperville with my mother. It was around that time Jackie and I lost touch."

"I tell you, Jackie was sick to be tired when you guys lost touch with us. Hold on for a second." Mike reaches into his pocket for his cell phone. "I'll give you our home phone number. And here's Jackie's cell phone number and here's mine."

"I won't lose you guys this time, I promise," Pat says.

"I don't think Jackie will allow it."

After they exchange numbers, she continues.

"Anyway, after Tony left Nam he was stationed in Hawaii on the island of Oahu —now I really loved that tour. The kids and I had a blast there." She can see that he is sweating and grabs him by the arm. "Let's step into the gym and get out of this heat."

"Let's do that," he replies.

"We'll bring each other up to date, and you can be reintroduced to some of our old friends," she says.

They walk toward the gym and she asks him, "Do you remember when Tony pulled David's pants down right there in the parking lot?"

"I remember it as if it just happened. It was right after David pulled my pants down to my knees," Mike says. "You have no clue how this place has brought back so many memories just by sitting in the car. I feel I've relived my youth in just a few minutes."

They walk into the gym and sign in, and then walk to a table where Pat recognizes some of her old friends. Mike sees Jimmy Tanner (Twin One) and James Tanner (Twin Two), and shakes their hands. He finds the mood a lot more welcoming than he anticipated.

Susan Wells looks at Mike in disbelief.

"I can't believe it, after all these years you returned."

He looks at her with a raised eyebrow.

"What I mean is you missed all the other reunions," she says. "I've been to every one of them since the tenth school reunion. I helped put all but the first one together. By the way, I know this is about fifty years late, but I am so very sorry for how we treated you back then."

"I accept your apology, but it really isn't necessary," Mike says. "When Jackie and I left we put all that behind us and focused on our life together. God has been very good to us; we have four children, and after we retired in '85, Jackie started writing and is now an accomplished author of over twelve books. And to keep me busy these days, I started a small nursery over fifteen years ago."

"Well, I just wanted you to know that I'm sorry," she says.

He reaches over and pinches her hand.

"Ouch," she squeals, looking at him and leaning away. "What was that for?"

"Before we all leave this gym tonight, you won't remember it even happened. That's the way God works in our lives. If we are willing to allow him to help us put our past in the past along with all the pain we have endured, we wouldn't remember half of it. Time will help heal and take the pain away. I'm not saying we'll forget everything that happened, but we won't feel the pain anymore. It may take a little while, but the sooner you let it go, the sooner the pain and anguish can start the healing process."

She wipes her eyes and quietly says, "I wish that was true for me."

"It's true for everyone," Mike says. "Jesus didn't just go about laying His hands on the sick and all is well for everyone. There was then and is today those He comes to and He asks of them one thing: 'Do you want to be healed?' You see, you have to want to be healed; you can't just sit in self-pity looking for life to all of a sudden change. You have to get up and start in the direction you're looking to go. You can't look at yesterday's problems and say today won't be any different. Everyday has the promise to be different, and it starts with you."

She looks up at the ceiling and says, "I used to pray, but it was about as useless as a three dollar bill in a shopping spree."

He laughs and tells her, "Just because you prayed and got no results doesn't mean you didn't get an answer."

Pat asks, "Could you explain that?"

"In the book of Daniel chapter 10 it says that Daniel fasted and prayed for over twenty-one days and got no answer. God sent his angel Gabriel to let him know that his prayers were heard the first day he prayed, and an answer was sent. But because the enemy came and fought against him, it took twenty-one days to get to him. We shouldn't give up because we don't get the answer when we expect it. God hears our prayers the first day, but the devil will do his best to do two things. First, he delays the answer for as long as it takes, and second, he discourages the one in prayer and causes them to give up and walk away from the answer. But it's there if you trust God, and you have to stay the course."

"Are you a minister now?" Susan asks.

"No I'm not, just one who stayed the course and endured youth with bloody noses, headaches, and humiliation. I prayed every day, and when I knew that I was about to get clobbered, or humiliated, I could go through a prayer faster than you can blink. It seemed to be all for naught at the time, but I just had to wait until I graduated and left this place before I got an answer."

Everyone standing around listening is silent. Jimmy breaks the silence and says, "I think he answered your prayers long before that."

"How do you figure that?" Mike asks. "From where I stood it took until the day I left this place."

"Did it?" Jimmy says.

Everyone is looking at Jimmy now.

"Would you like to enlighten us?" Pat remarks.

"One name," says Jimmy. "Tony. God sent you Tony."

Pat stands there with her hands over her mouth, holding her breath as tears begin to fall from her eyes.

"There were many times God had him step in for you. Tony was the only one nobody messed with in those days, and God made him your best friend."

Mike put both hands over his eyes and prayed a silent prayer, asking God to forgive him for not seeing the gift he was given. He pulled his hands down from his face and wiped the tears away.

Jimmy continues, "There are times we can't see the gifts we're given because we're focused on everything else. I'm no minister, but when I was in Korea and in Vietnam, it seemed when I was in the face of death my eyes were suddenly opened, and it was then I trusted those who God sent my way. More than once someone saved my life, even the enemy who was running at me with his bayonet out in front of him. I was on one knee when my rifle jammed, and I was about to stand up and use it as a club, when he stepped in front of a bullet I knew was meant for me. Sometimes Mike, even the best of us just don't see what's right in front of us."

"I'm sorry," Mike says, giving Jimmy a hug, "Thank you."

Janet Mars softly grabs Susan's arm and asks, "Susan, would you like to pray?"

"I'll think about it," Susan answers.

"Maybe later," Janet says.

"Yes, maybe later," she replies.

"Why don't we get caught up?" Mike suggests.

"Let's do that," says Jimmy.

They all find a seat, and Pat starts first. "Well before I make up for lost time, Mike was telling me how my good friend Jacquelyn is doing these days. She's doing very well and will be surprised to hear from me. He said she just didn't want to make this trip."

Elizabeth Grace interjects, "Well I can understand. I almost didn't make the trip myself."

Pat looks at Mike and says, "Of course you're probably wondering why Tony didn't make the trip."

"I was wondering," he says.

"Well long story real short," she begins, "after thirty years in the Army he retired, and two years after his retirement he was diagnosed with cancer. He passed away the following year."

"I'm sorry to hear that," Mike consoles. The others around Pat do the same.

She looks at them all and says, "Oh, we enjoyed our life together. We have seven children, four boys and three girls, along with seventeen grandchildren and twelve great-grandchildren. He lived long enough to see most of the grandchildren, and that was a blessing. We got the chance to travel all over the world with seven children in tow, and I tell you I wouldn't change a single day."

There are others with similar stories, and a couple who married six times while Susan Wells has never married once. They meet with more of their classmates and talk about the years after high school, showing off pictures of their children, grandchildren, and great-grandchildren.

Mike and the men leave the company of the women and band together at another table. "Well how in the world are you, Mike?" asks Twin One.

"I'm fine as I can be," he replies. "How about you?"

"Not bad for sixty-eight," he tells him.

"Who still lives here in Thumperville?" Mike asks.

"Not many of us. Twin and I live in Dallas, Bradley Dunbar still lives here, and you remember James Green, David's younger brother, don't you? Well he lives in Galveston; he was here for the fortieth reunion, but I see he didn't make this one. Wesley Edger moved to Houston, Ronald Everett lives in Georgia..."

"Wow," Mike jumps in. "That must be the farthest of us all, right?"

"Actually no, Andrew Johnson here lives in Alaska," points Bradley.

"I don't blame him for coming here; he's here to thaw out," says Jimmy.

"It's a beautiful country out there," Andrew claims.

"I prefer to see it from the comforts of my TV," Ronald states.

"Believe it or not, old sourpuss sitting over there moved to El Paso after his third marriage failed. He must have kids all over this state and Mexico," says Bradley.

"I see he prefers to eat alone," remarks Jimmy.

"Let him," says James. "I can only imagine what's going on in his mind right now."

"I don't want to know," says Jimmy. "Best to let sleeping dogs sleep, I always say."

"Sleeping dogs *lie*," James corrects him.

"No," says Jimmy. "If a dog is sleeping, he won't see you sneaking by his yard, but if he's awake and sees you trying to sneak by, it's more than likely you won't pass his yard without him coming after you."

"Let him sleep," the others agree, laughing.

"Speaking of Craig and all the children he has across the state, it all started with Susan over there." Bradley points at her, and everyone is looking in the direction of the women's table. "She had four children for him and took what you left behind, one beating after another until he kicked her out into the streets with all four of the kids to marry some woman from Las Vegas. Susan moved in with her parents for a little while."

"Yeah, but that marriage lasted less than a year," Bradley interjects. "She took flight after he beat her the first time, and his third marriage ended after one beating too many when she boiled some water and grease and poured it on him while he was asleep, and hightailed it out of there."

"Ohhhhh!" shout most of the men.

"I bet he sleeps with one eye open these days," says Andrew.

"Good for her," Mike says.

"Yeah well, he was in the hospital for a while for that, and then he moved to El Paso," says Bradley. "Susan moved to Oklahoma with the kids and now she's the director of some big company up there. She comes back for every reunion and helps put them together."

"That and to let old sourpuss see what he tossed to the curb," Andrew boasts.

"Why does he come here?" Mike asks.

Everyone at the table looks at one another and shrugs their shoulders, for they have no answer.

"So where's Mr. David Green?" asks Mike, changing the subject.

"Well he got himself in a bad fix back in '52, when he got into a shootout after robbing a bank in Dallas. He spent some time in the prison hospital, and then tried to escape. That got him sent to Huntsville State Prison and locked up in a dark cell. No one has heard from him since," says Andrew.

"If anyone's life was predictable after graduating, his was it," remarks Bradley.

"Did he even graduate?" James asks.

"No, and I do remember he was voted most likely not to succeed." They get a good laugh from that.

"Hey Mike, do you remember Coach Webb?" asks Bradley.

"Yes I do, and boy did he and Coach Grey make my life miserable in school. Neither man ever allowed me to join any of the team sports, even after I did all that running to make the track team."

"Kind of sounds like we should have called you Rudolph the Red-Nosed Reindeer," says Jimmy. Everyone laughs.

Bradley continues. "Yes, well he just celebrated his ninety-sixth birthday over at the nursing home down the road a bit. You should go and see him; he never believed you would ever return. Out of all of us, Mike, you are the one he talks most about, and not in a bad way I tell you. Pat used to come home with her kids and tell everybody how well you and Jacquelyn were doing. Coach Webb often said he wished he treated you a little better, and then he would say, 'Those were the times they lived in. Only the toughest were allowed to participate in sports.'"

"That's not true. Some of the schools we played against had players that looked like Mike on them, no offense," Jimmy says.

"None taken," Mike replies. "Maybe I will go and congratulate him on his ninety-sixth birthday. That's a blessing to live that long."

Ronald Everett looks at Mike. "You had to deal with a lot growing up here. Any of your kids as skinny as you were?"

Mikes laughs and says, "Only all of them, but they managed to impress the coaches. All three boys and my daughter participated in middle and high school sports."

"You know, after you and Tony left this place it got really quiet for a while, and then it seemed like everybody decided to leave," Ronald remembers. "The twins joined the Air Force and

Army, James Green and Wesley Edger joined the Navy, and I joined the Army."

"I called it the jailbreak," says James.

"I couldn't let all the glory go to Tony, Twin, and what was that guy's name who joined the Army after Tony left?" Ronald asks.

Jimmy looks down and says, "He was on the track team."

Then Mike says, "You wouldn't be speaking of Joey Kemp, would you?"

"No, not Joey. He married Lucy over there, and they had what... twelve children?"

"Holy smoke," Mike says as he leans back in his seat. "Twelve?"

"Twelve," Ronald replies.

Jimmy whistles through his teeth and shakes his head.

"Of course he's not here." Says Bradley. "because he passed away about four years ago. Same with Wesley Edger; the reason he's not here is because he was killed in Nam onboard one of the swift boats patrolling a narrow canal along the Mekong Delta, and..."

"Donald Westler!" Jimmy shouts as he remembers. "He joined the army right after Tony did, and then Ronald here joined right after him. I tell you, the military was the ticket out of this place for many of us."

After talking for an hour, Craig decides to invite himself to join the women's conversations. He acts like he does not see Susan sitting at the end of the table next to Pat, and says, "I didn't see your husband... what's his name?"

Pat looks at him with scalding eyes and says, "His name is Anthony Reams Sr., and that's Command Sergeant Major

Anthony Reams if you want to be specific. And if you need to know, he served his country for thirty years as a highly decorated soldier in the US Army. Now, if that's not enough for you to reel in your line, he passed away in '83."

"I guess that's something you're proud of," he remarks.

"Very proud," she replies. Pat just stares at him with her arms folded, waiting for the next insult.

Janet asks, "Are you through fishing yet? I think you should pack up your tackle box and move to a different fishing hole."

He stands there with a smirk on his face, and after they show him little attention, he walks over to where Mike and the guys are talking with a plate of meatballs and sausage. "Hey!" shouts Mike and the others as he walks up. "It's about time you joined the group. How's life been treating you?"

"Absolutely wonderful, gentlemen. I was wondering why Tony didn't show up… Pat tells me that he passed away in '83. Looking at Mike, I guess that means you don't have your protector here to help you now, do you?"

"Those days are long gone, Craig," James says. "We were all kids then, and now we're just a bunch of old men reminiscing about old times. If you want to behave like an eighteen-year-old bully, then you can go back over there and sit by your old cantankerous self."

"Craig," Mike calls, "why in the world do you want to behave like this? You're seventy years old, so you should be enjoying the time you have left with your family, not behaving like some adolescent teen."

Craig's face hardens. He curses Mike and the others, saying, "I don't need none of you old hens to tell me how I should be living my life. Especially this skinny, no-count doofus."

"Craig," Mike responds, "you have me mixed up with that kid you knew back in the forties, and I have no intention of getting into an argument with you."

At that time, all the ladies have stopped talking and the men begin to walk away. Craig curses Mike and stares at him from across the table. Jealously, he says, "Your retirement is a joke, and the life you're living is superficial at best. You think I didn't see you in the parking lot, you boneless coatrack? You were a pathetic janitor's son then, and you still are today."

Twin One taps Mike on the shoulder and tells him, "Don't allow yourself to be drawn into a confrontation with this old fool. Let's go." He motions for Mike to follow him and the others to another table.

Mike stands up straight, takes a deep breath, smiles, and starts to turn and walk away when Craig grabs one of the meatballs from his plate and throws it at Mike, hitting him in the face and knocking his glasses off. With meat sauce in his eye, Mike furiously yells at Craig, "You ignorant buffoon!" and bends down to pick up his glasses. Pat picks up his glasses for him, grabs a handful of napkins from the table, and finds a glass of water to help get the sauce out of his eye.

Jimmy and the others shout at Craig, "What is your problem?"

James goes to the men's room with Mike so that he can wash his face and clean himself up. Craig laughs and shouts at Mike, "While you're in there, toilet boy... clean it." Still laughing, he tosses a sausage into the air and attempts to catch it in his mouth. The sausage lodges in his throat instead, and he starts choking and immediately struggles to breathe. Craig turns around grabbing his throat; he falls over the tables, crashing and falling to the floor on his knees, gasping for air.

Still conscious, his eyes roll back as he fights to breathe, swinging and kicking widely at anyone coming near him trying to help. Susan calls the ambulance, and everyone stands around staring down at him.

In the madness of his mind, day becomes night, and millions of stars begin floating around his head. Then begin the whispers that seem to echo in his ears. With bloodshot eyes, and still swinging and kicking wildly, the room spins and the words "Rock, Paper, Scissors" begin to echo clearer in his mind. Then the game gets louder, *Rock, Paper, Scissors*... and louder,

Rock, Paper, Scissors.

More books by J. Lew

Novel
The Witches and Wizards of Ozz – *Deep Impact*

Coming Soon
Red Beans and Rice with Cornbread
Sepulcher – *The Devils Den*

Children's books - Chris Adventure books
I'm Not Afraid of The Dark
Sunken Treasures

Soon to be released
Little Ranch Hands
Chris's Family Vacation at Rocket World

We would like to hear from you
____

Visit our website at:
www.jlew-books.com

www.ingramcontent.com/pod-product-compliance
Lightning Source LLC
Chambersburg PA
CBHW051711180726
48283CB00004B/1297